Magar Invasion

Magar Invasion

...

Dr. Peter Gletzakos

ISBN-13: 9781517641320
ISBN-10: 1517641322
Library of Congress Control Number: 2015916457
CreateSpace Independent Publishing Platform
North Charleston, South Carolina

Other books by Dr. Peter Gletzakos
Courage (2014)

Upcoming
Perceptions: The Unfettered Ramblings of an Altered
Reality (2016)

To my nephew, Mathew.
The battle never ends…

Acknowledgements

• • •

I WOULD LIKE TO THANK Aly Cutkomp and Yiannis Gazis for their input and patience during the writing of this book. Their feedback was greatly valued and respected. It was nice to be able to bounce ideas off them and get an honest response and opinion, even though they knew I would fire them if they disagreed with me. Although we disagreed more than we agreed, I believe the final product would not be what it is, had it not been for their contribution.

I would like to thank John D. Townsend of Town's End Books for his early read and editing advice. A specialist antiquarian book dealer, he is part of a dying breed. A champion of the written word, he is both a gentleman and a master of his trade.

Special thanks go out to Kearen Enright for her amazing work on the cover of this book. She was also the artist extraordinaire behind my previous book "Courage". Her artistic prowess is truly admirable and greatly appreciated.

And finally to my wife, Mandy, and my daughter, Nataley, whose constant encouragement gets me past my "writer's block" moments and pushes me to finish what I started, I say thank you and I couldn't have done it without your help and support.

Prologue

● ● ●

"COME HERE, HUMAN," SAID A voice from his right.

Mathew froze. He was facing the alien supreme commander, General Moutari. He stood and stared, mouth agape, at the general. His excitement replaced with fear, he found himself glued to the floor.

"I said, '*Come here*'!" yelled the general. "Are you stupid? Did you not hear me?"

"I'm a-a sorry, sir," he said as he finally felt his feet moving.

"You will answer my questions, or I will shoot you into space through one of our plasma tubes. Do you understand?"

"Y-yes, sir."

"I want to know where the rebel hideout is."

"I—I don't know what you're talking about. I'm just a kid," he tried.

"Do not lie to me! You were caught running from our patrols. Where were you heading?" he demanded.

In that pivotal moment, gripped by fear and apprehension, Mathew made his decision. As if some divine power had suddenly filled him with courage and power, he decided not to give them any information, no matter what they did to him. He was angry. He was angry at himself for getting caught. He was angry that his mom was worried about him. He was angry at the aliens for invading his country and ruining their lives. But more importantly he was angry that they had killed all those people and especially his father. No matter what, he wasn't going to say a word, even at the cost of his life. But he would escape; he told himself, if the opportunity arose, so he could continue the fight.

• • •

CHAPTER 1

MATHEW STIRRED. *BANG! BOOM!* MATHEW'S eyes flew open as he felt his bed vibrate and heard his bedroom windows rattle. Could that be another alien ship landing so soon? *Bang! Boom!* There it was again. Mathew jumped from his bed. He threw back the curtains of his bedroom window, letting in the first rays of the morning. It looked to be another hot July day. No, it wasn't another alien ship landing, but it was their guns firing. The aliens were busy out in Boston harbor. Alien patrol boats were circling the piers like bees around a hive. Bright lights flashed in the early-morning light, like lighthouse beacons in a storm.

Jumping on one leg, trying to put his pants on while pulling on his tee shirt, Mathew was puzzled. The alien ship had been here for over a month. Three new ships had joined it about a week ago. Smaller in size, they came loaded with alien soldiers and equipment. A very scary sight. Ever since the invasion, Mathew was on edge like everyone else, not knowing what to expect next. Even a slight change from the norm was grounds for concern.

The scene below was surreal. His city was destroyed, laying in ruin. Hundreds of alien invaders were patrolling the streets, killing and harassing the city's survivors. Threatening and intimidating as they marched throughout the city, they carried all kinds of weapons. Their ships observed and supported ground troops, firing missiles to disperse crowds and "agitators" when necessary.

The ships could only be described as massive. Even the smaller crafts dwarfed anything humans had. The mother ship was just enormous. It took up at least half of Logan Airport, where it currently resided. The ship was so large you could see it from any spot in the city, and Boston was a large city. It was a cross between the *Millennium Falcon* from the Star Wars movies and the *Cylon Battleship* from the television series *Battlestar Galactica*. It was so huge it had two drop ships attached to it. The smaller ships were just as impressive. Their long lines and sleek angles gave them speed and maneuverability. Capable of carrying tremendous amounts of aliens and equipment, these were no slow cargo haulers plodding along the atmosphere at a snail's pace. They were ultra-prime fighting machines, traveling at warp speeds, delivering death and destruction with minimal effort and maximum effect.

Mathew remembered the speed with which they buzzed through the sky the night of the invasion. The nerd in him still marveled at the technology that allowed such velocity and the capability and accuracy needed to stop and land on a dime.

From Mathew's elevated vantage point, the ships looked to be elongated triangles with discernible wings that housed extremely large engines and what looked like thrusters the size of 747's. Armaments of all sorts and varieties, many he'd never seen before, adorned the aircraft's outer skin, like Christmas ornaments on a tree. Rapid-fire lasers, plasma weapons, all the size of army tanks, were scattered throughout the body of the alien vessels.

The biggest weapons were a pair of missile launchers situated on the mother ship just below the bridge window. They consisted of four large tubes the size of submarines. They fired nuclear harpoon missiles equipped with solid propellant rocket motors. The advanced alien guidance systems with thermal and radar sight allowed the operator to track missiles from launch to impact. The long-range missiles could penetrate just about anything Earth's military had. If the nuclear heads were detonated, whole planets could be obliterated in seconds. What Mathew assumed were stabilizers littered the underbelly of the crafts. Even as far away as he was, he could feel, more than hear, a constant humming he assumed was the ship's nuclear reactor power sources. The ships didn't rest on any wheels, struts, or other landing gear that he could see, but floated several feet above ground. The mother ship looked as if it were resting on the airport's buildings and planes that were on the runways, when it had conveniently landed on top of them.

BANG!

Mathew froze; his breath caught in his throat. Standing still, half-dressed, he could see smoke rising from across the water. Another pocket of resistance destroyed, he thought. It was happening more and more frequently, ever since the new ships had arrived and deployed their soldiers and weapons. Resistance groups were no match against advanced intergalactic weapons.

Boom, boo-oo-oom! His bedroom windows shook. Losing his balance, Mathew fell to the floor, making enough noise to notify his mother he was up. Scrambling to stand, Mathew heard his mother inquire about the noise he just made.

"Mathew, Mathew, are you okay? What was that noise?" she asked.

"Nothing, Mom. I'm okay," he said, rubbing his bruised rear end. He had fallen on one of his old roller-blades, and the hard plastic wheels had done a job on his behind. He really should clean his room, he thought as he kicked the offending rollerblade under his bed, stubbing his toe in the process.

Angry with himself for his clumsiness, he ran to his door and flung it open. Running down the hall, he found his mother standing in the kitchen. She stood, white-faced, a cup of coffee strangled I her white-knuckled hands.

"Oh, good morning. I didn't see you standing there. Are you hungry? Do you want breakfast?" she asked, forcing a smile and trying to hide her worry over the explosions.

"No thanks, Mom, just some juice."

While she went to the fridge, Mathew peeked out the window. They were on the fourth floor of a six-floor building and had a pretty good view of the whole North

End of Boston, as well as the wharf and surrounding piers. The view had improved considerably after the alien attack. Eighty percent of the city was destroyed, with most buildings lying in heaps of concrete and twisted metal. Few remained standing, his building being one of the lucky ones.

As his mom poured juice into a glass, she remarked, "They must have found quite a few resistance cells. I heard at least five loud explosions in the past two hours." Resistance cells or not, the aliens are infamous for their shoot first, ask questions later mentality, she thought to herself as she handed Mathew his drink.

Mathew covertly observed his mother, a pretty lady in her early forties. With striking black eyes and long black hair tied back behind her ears, his mom could still pass for a college coed. She was dressed in jeans and an old shirt of his father's. She was wearing sneakers, and a baseball cap sticking out of her back pocket. Even though she hadn't been assigned to a specific work detail by the invading forces, she left every day, scavenging food and supplies. She also took time to help neighbors who were too old, too ill, or too injured. Supplies were in high demand. Everything from food to medical goods was in short supply. The aliens controlled all goods, and you needed the vouchers that they supplied on a monthly basis to access them. Everything from food to personal hygiene products was meagerly metered out.

Weeks after the initial attack and subsequent invasion, the most "industrious" of the remaining citizens went into business supplying necessary goods to the rest of the survivors. They formed a kind of underground co-op, where people could obtain supplies ranging from clothes to canned goods. If you didn't have the necessary vouchers for your needs, you could always frequent the underground black market, bartering or paying money or other valuables for whatever you desired. Black marketeers roamed the streets and camps, peddling their wares, charging exorbitant fees for things they salvaged from the wreckage of buildings and stores. With the majority of the world destroyed, with less than twenty percent of the population alive, people still pursued the almighty dollar. The aliens allowed the underground enterprise to continue as another means of pacifying the remaining population. The one thing they didn't allow was the selling of any type of weapons. If they found out that weapons were exchanging hands, they would kill the participants and leave their corpses behind as a warning.

"I hope the resistance is killing some of the aliens," Mathew said hotly, turning back to the window, making believe he didn't see his mother's tears. He was thinking of his deceased father and the scores of friends and relatives who hadn't survived the attacks.

He knew she thought about his father, too. His dad had been killed during the initial invasion, eleven months ago. His parents were having dinner at a waterfront restaurant, celebrating their anniversary. Flying out of the clouds, their weapons blazing, the aliens destroyed half the city in minutes. His father, strafed with shattered glass and bullets, died instantly. His mom had been thrown under a table by the blast that rocked the restaurant. Confused, hurt, and bleeding from multiple cuts and scrapes, she made her way back to their apartment. Hysterical with grief and worry for her son's safety, she fought the fleeing masses, explosions, and fires to return. She found Mathew cowering in a hall closet, a phone in his hands and tears in his eyes.

"Mom," he screamed, "What's happening? Where's Dad?" he asked. Dropping the useless phone, he ran into her arms, hugging her tightly, not wanting to let go.

Grabbing him firmly, she sobbed uncontrollably. "He's gone, Mathew. Daddy's dead."

"What? Why? What happened to Dad? What's going on? What were all those explosions?" Mathew asked hysterically, never having seen his mom in this condition before.

"I don't know, honey. As crazy as it sounds, it looks like an alien invasion. We have to get out of here and find some shelter, preferably underground," she replied. Composing herself the best she could, she released Mathew and sprang into action, urging him to do the same. "Hurry, Mathew. Grab whatever you think we might need and throw it in your backpack. I'll get some food and water and a flashlight; you grab some clothes and the medical kit and anything else you can think of. We need to hurry."

Equipped with supplies, they made their way to the building's basement. As they reached this lower level, they were swallowed up in a sea of neighbors and strangers.

Everyone was screaming and crying, wondering what was going on. No one had any answers.

They stayed in that basement for several weeks. Every couple of days, several people would leave their little asylum to go above ground, seeking food, water, and information. Information started to trickle in. They had been invaded by an alien race that was working its way toward total domination. The aliens were slowly moving across the country, killing the military, as well as our civilian population. Any resistance was quickly suppressed with intense firepower. Anyone who didn't surrender was considered an enemy and was eliminated. Many people were shuffled into prison camps where alien guards kept a close eye on them, but most were terminated with extreme prejudice.

It didn't take long for the government to surrender. The military laid down its arms, and our president made a national announcement declaring surrender to the Magar race. His speech was broadcast from the alien ships over and over. This was because they had destroyed all broadcasting facilities, satellites, and telecommunications. No phones, no internet, no television. Even shortwave radio was inoperable. The populace was left in the middle of a communications blackout. It was a return to the dark ages.

The president said the country was now under Magar control. "Please return to your homes. We were to stay calm and not resist. These are trying times, but necessary to avoid total extinction. Further instructions will be forthcoming."

People slowly started to emerge from the rubble. Dazed and disoriented, they tried to return to their homes, find their families, and figure out a way to survive. Many were forced to live together in shelters or seek refuge at friends' and families' homes, if theirs were destroyed. The carnage was unbelievable. Many just wandered the streets, looking for people they were never going to find. Rumors put the death toll at over two hundred and fifty million. Over two-thirds of America's population had been slaughtered in a matter of days. Not much was known about the rest of the world. People whispered that whole countries were wiped completely off the map. With communications being as compromised as they were, you didn't know what or who to believe. There were days when there was no electricity or water. Pretty soon people had trouble finding food and supplies and started to fight among themselves. Others tried to curry favor with the alien race reporting on their friends and neighbors. They turned in friends and acquaintances for the smallest of offenses. You didn't know who to trust.

The one constant was the roving patrols of aliens. They came in all shapes, but only in large sizes. Taller than most humans, heavily armed and armored, they traveled in groups. Greenish black mottled skin peeked beneath alien bulletproof leather padding; broad lupine faces held mandibles sporting extremely sharp teeth. Bloodshot eyes resided below large sloped helmeted heads. They were the warrior class from a world far far away. Hands with six fingers gripped alien weaponry as well as human armament.

Large guns, pistols, plasma rifles, and automatic weapons out of comic books and wild imaginations were carried. Even knives and swords were commonplace. They would accost people on the street and break into people's shelters looking for what they referred to as "illegal" weapons. They would punish any insubordination or rebelliousness quickly and severely, many times leaving corpses in their wake, especially if "illegal" weapons were found.

• • •

"DISOBEDIENCE WILL BE PUNISHED!!!" THIS was blared this over and over from the alien ships as they patrolled the skies. These smaller torch ships could maintain high speeds indefinitely, thus enabling them to cover large distances in very short time. Loaded with all manner of weapons, from simple cannons to external heat-seeking missile armament and cluster bombs. Pulse wave weapons debilitated victim's motor and sensory innervations. The ships were often deployed to squelch unrest, rioting, and protests. Many times they just flew fast and low to the ground, the back draft of their engines dispersing crowds and clearing areas the size of football fields. They also acted as air support for ground troops during battles and skirmishes with some of our remaining forces.

After several months, things started to calm down. Work crews were formed to help clear the damage and the electricity came back on full time. Even though there was no phone coverage, internet or television, the aliens re-opened food and water supply lines and provided desperately needed medical care. Life started to return to some normalcy. That is if you can call living under alien rule normalcy.

As people got over the shock the invasion had caused, they became angry. Resistance and discord brewed among the survivors. Resistance cells attacked the Magars more and more frequently. The Magars increased their patrols as well as their numbers in our area. When they encountered any sort of dissension they were quick to squash it without leniency.

"Disobedience will be punished," blasted the alien shuttles as they hovered above the city.

All of a sudden a door slammed and there was a sound of running feet and knocking at the door. Mother and Mathew looked at each other, as they headed to the door of their apartment.

A voiced called, "Mathew! Mathew! Did you hear the guns?"

Opening the door, mother and son found Molly looking at them with an expectant expression.

"Molly?" they both said at the same time. Molly was Mathew's close friend from down the hall. She had been in all of Mathew's classes since his family had moved into this section of the city. They had moved into the North End of Boston five years ago when his father left the military for a job as head of security for a big financial firm downtown. At the time his mother was a teacher at the school on Prince Street.

Mathew loved living here. He loved the people, his school, his friends, and especially all the delicious food just outside his door. The streets were narrow and compact and some days so full of locals and tourists he could barely move. He appreciated the abundant history of the area. A self-proclaimed history buff ever since he could read, Mathew frequented the Old Church, Paul Revere's house, the Freedom Trail, and all the old cemeteries and burial grounds. They were his virtual 3-D books. His neighborhood was packed with Italian restaurants, his favorite cuisine. He had roamed every nook and cranny throughout the years, knew all the colorful locals and the best places to get pizza and gelato.

Faneuil Hall was his favorite place in the world. Bordered by Government Center, Haymarket, the North End, and the waterfront, it was a huge 250-year-old marketplace, bursting with restaurants, shops, live street performers, and all kinds of crazy people. He had spent hours exploring on his own and especially with Molly and his best friend, Dillon. They had gone into every establishment, large and small. They ran through alleys, up and down countless stairs, through residential and commercial buildings, in one door and out another. They knew vendors, street performers, and security guards by name. They could tell you how to get from Commercial Street to Hanover Street in less than ten minutes or which bridge to take to get to the South End depending on the time of day. If they weren't in school or doing homework, they were out gallivanting, exploring the city, making friends, and finding the best places to satisfy their hunger pangs.

His and Molly's parents had grown close over the years. They traveled and spent countless holidays together. Lately, Molly was spending more and more time in their apartment, as her parents were assigned to a cleanup detail and were nervous about leaving her alone.

"She can stay with us when you're out," my mother had offered. "It's the least we could do after all the love and support you've shown us, especially since my Alex' passing. I don't know what we would have done without you."

Those were a tough couple of months after his father died. If not for Molly's and Dillon's parents, things would have definitely spiraled out of control. Stricken with grief over the loss of her husband and the chaos that ensued, Mathew's mother became mentally and emotionally lost. She would take to the streets, looking for something she couldn't define. Some days she roamed the streets, heedless of the danger the alien's presence or human predators presented. Even though she did her best to take care of her son, she was just going through the motions. Often times, as she left their apartment, Mathew wondered if he would see her again. Although wallowing in his own grief, Mathew tried to be strong for her. He tried to make every meal, no matter how meager or bland, seem like a gourmet feast, but she ate less and less, and her gaunt features mirrored her wounded soul. She would tell him she just wasn't hungry, that she was fine, or remind him how much she loved him. Many times he expressed his concern with her "walks" as she called them, but she assured him she was all right and just needed some air. Still, Mathew worried about her and would follow her without her knowing, making sure she was okay and no harm came to her. He watched as she roamed the city, scavenging food and water for them. She would stop and stare at ruined buildings or the burned-out, mangled remnants of cars and buses. At those moments, he knew she was trying to find her way back from her dark pit of despair. He would watch with a broken heart as silent tears flowed down her cheeks and quiet sobs racked her too-thin body. Slowly those long walks proved therapeutic, and with the help and support of their friends, they both emerged from their sorrow, physically unscathed. As the months passed, they found the strength to deal with the pain and return their lives to some semblance of order and routine.

Molly stood in the hallway, trying to get a look through their window at the spaceships flying around. "Mathew, did you hear all those explosions? They've been going off for hours. What's happening? Do you think it's the resistance? Do you think any aliens have gotten killed? Can you see anything out your windows? I don't think my parents are going to work today."

"Easy there, motor-mouth. Take a breath before you pass out from the lack of O2. And get in here. You're causing a scene again," Mathew joked.

"Mathew, be nice," chided his mother from behind him. "Good morning, Molly. How are you?"

"Good morning, Mrs. Holloway. I'm fine, and you?" Molly said with a big smile, reflecting the admiration and fondness she felt for his mom.

Mathew realized that every door on the floor was open with occupants trying to see what all the commotion was. Neighbors stuck their heads out of their apartments and started asking one another questions. Wheezing and coughing an older gentleman made his way out of his apartment.

"Mr. Marks!" Mathew shouted. "You should be in bed." He ran to the old man's side, offering him his arm for support. Mr. Marks had been battling pneumonia for the past month. One of the roving doctors told them that he should be in bed till he came back to check up on him. Mathew and his mom were taking care of the old guy, but he was a handful. Half the time Mathew and his friends would run into him on the street, observing the alien patrols. When they tried to get him back home, he would croak, "I'm fine. A little cold isn't enough to put me in a grave. If the Russians couldn't do it, then Mr. Strept O'Coccus didn't stand a chance." His cackle usually turned into a phlegm-coated coughing fit.

Mathew's dad had said that the "old codger" had worked for the CIA, and was instrumental in bringing down the "wall." Even though Mathew didn't know what that meant, he still liked the old guy and his stories about the old days before computers and all this "new-fangled" technology.

"The fools, the idiots!" he hollered as he made his way down the hall.

"Who? What's happening, Mr. Marks?" Molly asked.

"Why those crazy rebels are fighting the aliens again. Those aliens will kill them all, if they keep attacking them. They need a plan. They can't go off willy-nilly and expect to survive. They need a plan, I tell you!"

"Come in and have some breakfast, Mr. Marks," Mom offered, trying to calm him. "You must be hungry. You too, Molly. Mr. Marks can tell us his ideas over a good breakfast," she said, winking at Mathew and Molly as she escorted Mr. Marks into the apartment.

Although Mathew was hungry and wanted to eat, he didn't want to miss anything going on outside. In the kitchen the three sat at the table while Mathews's mom put breakfast together. Eggs and toast, ham and bacon, butter and jam, a veritable buffet. His mom had been lucky the past week; she'd happened upon a group of rebels that had stolen provisions from the aliens. Necessities such as water, soap, detergents, toilet paper, and most importantly foodstuffs were literally being thrown off the back of a U-Haul truck. At a time when they couldn't even procure the basics, this had been a godsend. They were parked just doors away from Mathew's building. His mother had rushed back home; loaded up with so many supplies; she'd make a packhorse jealous. She'd run up six flights of stairs, depositing her mammoth load before going back for more. Two trips later she was both exhausted and satiated. And being the woman she was, she shared the supplies with other members of the building and tried to feed as many friends as she could before anything spoiled and needed to be thrown out. She was such an open, caring, selfless person that people gravitated to her like bees to honey. Many times people would share their meager supplies with them, even when they didn't need them. His mother would always thank them for their kindness, exchange pleasantries, then proceed to give them something in return. She would then pass out anything they didn't need to people who did. That was the way current civilization, especially in the North End, functioned these days. For a moment, lost in his thoughts, Mathew almost forgot the battles and explosions raging outside.

"Well, Mr. Marks, I suppose you can tell us what's going on now," Mom said as she placed the food on the table. As they reached across to fill their own plates, Mr. Marks started his story.

"Not much to tell," mumbled Mr. Marks. "The rebels sneaked into an alien stronghold last night and blew up one of their spaceships. The Magars are going crazy. They are increasing their patrols, trying to catch the rebels responsible. It seems they somehow got their hands on some military-grade C-4 explosive and used it to destroy an alien spaceship. During the confusion the explosion caused, they were able to abscond with several truckloads of weapons and supplies. They even managed to kill a few dozen aliens in the process."

Mathew looked at Mr. Marks gravely. "You went out earlier than usual this morning. Did you see anyone or anything unusual?" He asked, hoping to glean some more information. He continued with, "Did you happen to know or suspect something like this would happen?" he asked eyeing the "old codger" closely to see if he could pick up any indication that the old dude knew something of the attack beforehand.

"Explosions woke me," he said, straight-faced. "They started before it was real light. I don't sleep good anyway, so once up, I decided to take a walk and see what was going on."

In the midst of a growth spurt, Mathew was stuffing himself mightily as he listened to Mr. Marks talk. He paid close attention as he reached for another piece of toast. It wasn't often the rebels struck a significant blow. Usually it was hit and run kind of stuff, causing more of a nuisance than any real damage. Something like this could breathe new life into the resistance movement.

The aliens were sure to be highly agitated and extremely aggressive over the next several days. People would have to step lightly and try not to draw undue attention to themselves, so as not to become collateral damage. The Magars would be out hunting the guilty parties hoping to make an example of them, so as to avoid future confrontations with the human populace. They were sure to exterminate anyone they thought guilty, for no other reason than to take out their frustrations and show what would happen if these rebel attacks continued.

What would the Supreme Commander do? Ever since he had arrived aboard the mother ship, the alien forces seemed more organized and definitely better armed. The first forces after the initial attacks were far more aggressive, causing pain, havoc and death just for fun. They hassled and harassed people, demeaning them, and causing physical pain whenever they felt like it. Even after the surrender was official, they continued their sadistic games. People were afraid to leave their homes and shelters for fear of being tortured and abused. Now with the appearance of their leader, the troops were more organized and had ceased their murderous ways, although they continued to pester and abuse people when the opportunity arose. It was said that the Supreme Leader was very impatient and vindictive. He would be extremely angry over these past events and would probably release his dogs to seek revenge.

"You think there'll be a battle, Mr. Marks?" Mathew asked excitedly.

"Battle? Why, young man, I do believe you'd like to get into a scrap or two yourself," he said, not quite hiding his grin behind a napkin. "I'll tell you what my father told me when I was your age: be careful what you wish for. I should know," he said with a faraway look in his eyes. "War is nothing to take lightly. People get hurt and more than not killed, as you well know. This isn't make-believe; this is the real deal."

BANG!

"That doesn't sound good," Molly said, wide-eyed, her food caught in mid swallow. Gulping she continued, "Do you think they're firing at humans?"

"'Course it doesn't. And, yes, they ain't firing for show. Magars are serious this time. They can't believe the rebels bypassed their security and destroyed their aircraft." Mr.

Marks said, clearly becoming agitated with all the questions hurled his way.

"The aliens are increasing their security at all their locations and probably calling in more troops. They mean business. I'm sure General Moutari, the Supreme Commander of the alien forces, has ordered his troops to ferret out the rebels and eliminate them using any means necessary. By the time we are done eating, those aliens will capture or kill those rebels and then proceed to turn the screws even tighter for the rest of us." Mr. Marks said this with such passion that pieces of food and spittle flew from his mouth.

Mom shook her head. "I don't know. Some of these so called rebels seem serious. They're ex-military and well trained. That business last night was no walk in the park. They were well organized and their plan successful. It was the most damage done to the Magars since they invaded our country."

"Oh, there's always a chance of success with surprise attacks. The problem is there are always hotheads who don't listen to anyone but themselves. They think they know what's best. Their plans lack substance and imagination. That gets people killed."

Boom, boo-oom!

This time the whole building shook. The lights flickered, and a bowl fell off the counter. The explosions were getting stronger, closer, and more intense. They all raced to the window and saw smoke rising two miles away. Alien aircraft were hovering in the sky. The waterfront and surrounding harbor was full of alien vessels. What looked like jet skis circled the pier and waterways. Single and double occupant, they barely touched the water as they patrolled their respective areas. Loaded with all manner of high-tech weaponry, they could sink any ocean vessel with minimal effort. These souped up alien water craft were right out of the 007 movies, capable of tremendous speed and limitless destruction.

"See what I mean?" Mr. Marks. "That's massive alien firepower. It makes the earth tremble. How can we hope to defeat something so strong?"

"Who are they firing at?" Molly wanted to know. "Surely the rebels would have evacuated the area by now. I wonder who the rebels are and where they came from."

"Upstate most likely. Some sort of army's been mustered up there," Mom added. "Mrs. Miller heard it from her sister who's visiting friends in that region. They're hiding out somewhere close to the shore in New Hampshire. They've been causing havoc up and down the coast and surrounding towns. They had some success because of the small contingent of alien forces, but I don't know how long that's going to last. I'm sure the aliens will send reinforcements there soon, especially now that their leader is on the scene."

"Upstate!" exclaimed Mathew. "That's only a couple hours away. Do you really think a whole rebel army has been raised?"

Mr. Marks replied, "I do, but calling it an army might be stretch. Probably a ragtag group of civilians and soldiers who survived the initial attacks. I'm sure there are a few good men and women, but there's sure to be some riffraff, stragglers, and malcontents hanging around, causing more problems than good. They probably have limited weapons and supplies."

"I agree with you," Mom said. Having been married to a former military man, she was smarter than most when it came to assessing certain situations and rumors. "It must be hard gathering supplies and weapons, especially while constantly moving around trying to avoid the alien patrols."

Mathew gulped and nearly choked on a mouthful of toast. The rebel army! They were the people's last resort, he thought to himself.

"Do you think it's the rebel army who attacked last night, Mr. Marks?" Mathew asked between bites, ignoring his mother's cautious interpretation.

"What? How should I know? They're probably fool enough. But they slipped up if they didn't get away in time. Nobody knows who's behind this latest attack. One thing you can be sure of, though, is that when General Moutari lays his hands on those rebels, they'll suffer, every last one of them," Mr. Marks said out loud, while secretly contemplating his soft bed. He'd clearly eaten too much, and after that morning walk, he was tired. He definitely wasn't a young pup anymore, he thought chuckling to himself, but he'd be damned if he'd let this young whippersnapper know how exhausted he was.

When breakfast was done, Mathew told his mom he was going out. Readying himself for his mother's concerned rejection of his statement; he casually made his way to the door, giving Molly a meaningful glance, hoping to enlist her help. By the look he got in return, he knew he was on his own. Why couldn't women just understand? He needed to know what was going on out there and he couldn't do that while sitting here. Anyway, the aliens weren't as concerned with kids and old people, he told himself. Look at Mr. Marks, the old dude was prancing around the area this morning during the peak of the conflict and nothing happened to him.

"I don't know if that's a good idea, Mathew. It's too dangerous today. Maybe you should stay in today while things settle down."

"I'll be fine, mom. You know I know the area like the back of my hand, plus I'll be extra careful, I promise. I just want to know what's going on," Mathew yelled as he ran out the door before anyone could say anything else.

"That boy better watch himself," mumbled Mr. Marks as Molly and his mom exchanged worried looks.

• • •

CHAPTER 3

MATHEW RAN THROUGH THE STREETS, dodging debris, people, and alien patrols. They were all over the place, questioning people and searching buildings. The Magars traveled in large groups carrying huge laser weapons and sporting angry scowls. People quickly moved out the way as they approached, hoping to avoid any collateral retribution. No matter how menacing the alien forces looked or how dangerous the environment was, there was an excited buzz in the air. The story was all over the city now. The rebel army had struck a blow against the invaders.

Mathew heard snatches of conversations as he ran.

"Why didn't they destroy more ships?"

"Just wait. They probably have more planned."

People had gathered on rooftops, staring off into the distance toward the harbor. He wished he could climb up to one of the roofs for a better view. He continued to run in that direction.

The alien guns were still firing, though at longer intervals, when Mathew reached an alley on the outskirts of the North End. With the sun moving higher and the day turning hot and humid, he tried to maintain his tempo. Before long he was breathing hard and sweating heavily. Still he kept up his fast pace. Eventually he started running a few yards, walking a few yards. This was an African-tribe style of covering ground. His father had shown him how it was done. His father had shown and taught him many things that were proving useful these past few months. The more time passed, the more he missed his father, but he didn't let his sorrow control him, like it once had. His father wouldn't want him to be morose and miserable. So he cherished his memory, and tried to recall all the little things. He had done so much with his father over the years that he had taken all their activities for granted. He had learned how to ski and sail, how to fire and take care of a gun, how to hunt and forage in the woods. They had gone hiking and swimming on the Cape, as well as clamming and fishing numerous times. Being in the military had taught his dad to constantly be active, and he had tried to pass this down to his son. He was always urging him to learn new things and constantly expand his horizons. "You never know what will happen. What you learn today might save your life tomorrow," he would constantly tell him. Little did he know how right he was, Mathew thought, feeling a sting in his eyes and a lump in his throat. All he could do now was try to make his father proud with his thoughts and actions.

Mathew cut across a side street and jumped a small fence. Black smoke was rising from behind a building up ahead. Was the rebel army still there? Mathew had to know. He had to. Continuing his trek around a huge bomb crater in the middle of the road, he watched people milling about. Cowed or content he couldn't tell. If it wasn't for the rebels and resistance, the human race would find itself extinct and not from the hostile invaders but from their own apathy, he thought.

Yes, we did get invaded by aliens and yes, the aliens did kick our butts all the way into the next decade but damn it, we are the best nation in the world. We have the greatest minds in the world. We have the best military and the most brilliant scientists. We are made up of smart, tough, persistent, and hugely determined individuals. So had people just given up and accepted their fate? Where was the fire and resolve that made this country great? We had fought and won wars, helped liberate countless countries from tyranny and oppression, put men on the moon, and drilled for oil and gas in the bottom of the ocean. Every time someone told us we couldn't do something, we tried even harder, until we proved them wrong. So why is it now when we needed to come together and break these alien chains, we sat on our hands and looked for others to help us? Were we so weak and pathetic that we were willing to suffer untold humiliation and degradation or are we just biding our time? Mathew wished with all his heart it was the second.

It was funny how clueless people could be sometimes. They assumed the rebels would be unsuccessful in their fight against the alien oppressors. They never once thought about joining the movement and fighting for their freedom. They trudged along, keeping their heads down, avoiding eye contact, hoping to avoid any sort of conflict. Content with their fate, they lived their lives under the radar. They didn't even know that there were people training in secret compounds and mountain hideouts located hours away. Training to fight for them, so they could preserve their right for apathy.

Mathew knew all about it, though. Several times he had visited one of the compounds with his friend Dillon. Other times he had gone on his own, hitching a ride from strangers traveling in the same direction. Although he was too young to take part in the drills, he was allowed to watch. This was due to the fact that Dillon's older brother, Brian, was one of the leaders. But this was the first time that an out-of-town rebel force had carried out an attack in the city. They mostly stayed away from the city because of the large amount of roving alien forces. Also the city was the unofficial headquarters of the invading alien race. Ever since General Moutari, Supreme Commander of the alien forces, had landed with his sizableforce, rebels had become personas non-gratas, as Luis, his neighbor, the Cuban exile living on the third floor used to say.

"You know, Mathew, I was persona non grata also, to Presidente Castro and his people back in Cuba, because I too wanted freedom for my people. I too was forced to abandon my home and family to avoid execution. I had been fighting for freedom for my country for years before these aliens invaded. Now, I don't even know if Cuba even exists. It wouldn't take much to obliterate a small island like that." He would often say, while painting a colorful description of his country and its people with his words and hand gestures. "Oppression is not good, Mathew; I saw what it can do. That is why I love this country so much. Here we live in a society based on individual freedoms and rights. Our laws and beliefs govern the way that we treat others and how others treat us. We are guaranteed certain rights under laws that are guaranteed by our government. One of these rights is to be treated fairly and not be subjected to cruel treatment or unjust punishment. We have the right to not be tortured or subjected to degrading treatment. Our rights protect us from racial and religious persecution. Everyone should be treated with respect and dignity even at time of war. And that is why the rebels mean so much to the survival of this great nation. They represent hope and maybe someday a rallying point for the people, in hopes of defeating these oppressors and sending them back to where they came from."

Mathew knew that Luis could go on like this for hours and hours. I guess that's what happens when you fight your whole life for a cause and then one day you wake up and find what you were fighting for no longer exists. Either way Mathew liked Luis a lot. It was refreshing to hear a Cuban accent among all the Italian in his small sphere. He especially enjoyed it when Luis pronounced Cuba as "Cuva."

"Hello, young man. Where are you off to in such a hurry?"

Startled, Mathew looked up into the steel-blue eyes of a tall man. The stranger had stepped out of a hidden doorway. In his mouth was an unlit cigarette that he chewed contentedly. In his hands was an AK-47 automatic rifle, just like the people in Dillon's brother's rebel group carried.

"I--I'm going to the harbor."

"The harbor? Why the harbor?"

"To see the rebel army," Mathew stuttered.

The tall man's eyes went wide. "Is that so? What makes you think the rebel army is at the harbor?"

Mathew hesitated. No knowing who folks were these days. He could have been an alien informer. Finally, he spoke cautiously, while preparing himself to run if things turned ugly. "People are saying the rebel army attacked the alien stronghold last night and blew up a spaceship!"

"Is that so? And who would be starting rumors like that?" he said with a glint in his eye. "I wouldn't believe everything you hear, son. The rebels are surely causing some trouble for the aliens, but I seriously doubt that they could cause that much damage with their limited arsenal. Half the time three rebels have to share the same bullet, and that's if they could get their hands on the gun the whole group shares," he said, laughing at his own joke.

When nothing more was said, Mathew turned to leave, but the man barred his way. "Better go back home, kid," he said gruffly but not unkindly. "It's too dangerous around here. You could get hurt or even worse, killed."

Mathew was on the verge of arguing when he heard the thunder of many boots on the ground. They were coming from the direction of the harbor. He also heard a large vehicle approaching from the same direction. As the noise grew louder, the man disappeared through the same doorway he had come out. "Get going," he called over his shoulder. But Mathew had already started running in the opposite direction. He ran headlong down a short alley and came out on a small dirty street he was unfamiliar with. Moving quickly, he turned down another alley. Following it to the end and came out onto a street he was familiar with. As he was about to take off toward the city, a large truck came barreling around the corner. Mathew jumped out of the way to avoid being hit but not before recognizing the driver. It was the tall man in an old World War II transport truck, complete with a canvas top, diesel engine, and antique license plates. The driver had taken the turn too fast and had to slow down to compensate. Mathew froze. Sounds of the alien patrol getting closer resonated. He fled, knowing he didn't have a choice. To escape getting caught, he had to follow the truck, but he discerned he wouldn't make it around the corner before the Magar patrol saw him.

CHAPTER 4

• • •

IT WAS TOO FAR. HE had to think! The truck!! If he could catch up to the truck and jump in the back! He ran as fast as his legs would carry him, but the truck was accelerating. He wasn't going to make it. Suddenly, a dog ran into the street right in front of the truck. The driver slammed on the brakes. That was all Mathew needed to catch up to the truck. Reaching and grabbing a hanging chain, he hoisted himself up and over the half door. Falling into the back, he lay there, catching his breath. His heart was exploding. Drenched in sweat, he lay flat, struggling to breathe and return his pulse back to a safe rhythm. He was too young to have a heart attack, he mused.

When he had caught his breath, Mathew peeked out the back. The truck had crossed onto Commercial Avenue and was slowly moving through the city, avoiding craters, potholes, burned out abandoned cars, and innocent civilians. There was no sign of that alien patrol but armed aliens lined the road. Mostly in groups of two and three, they were moving toward the harbor. Nobody seemed in command. There was no orderly marching. They just seemed to be moving in the same direction. Maybe the rebels had caused more disorder and confusion than was previously thought. Nobody stopped the truck.

A few minutes later, the truck made its way into Charlestown. The houses looked empty and deserted, but the streets were full of people. Confusion reigned everywhere. People were shouting questions and yelling at each other. One man was waving a gun in the air, but nobody paid him any attention.

As the truck slowed to avoid running over the people, Mathew slid over the truck's tail gate. Landing on the street, he was quickly swallowed up in the press of sweaty, smelly bodies. Some glanced at him curiously, but most didn't even pay attention to him. There were people everywhere, men, women, children, young, and old. Some were carrying weapons; others just had sticks or nothing at all. They were heading in the same direction, but each at their own pace. Some traveled in groups, others alone, some moved quickly while others seemed to be taking their time visiting with friends or acquaintances. If he didn't know better, he'd have thought it was a parade or festival the area was so well known for.

Mathew approached a group of people who were lounging near a fallen brick wall. "Excuse me," Mathew said hesitantly. "Can you tell me what's going on?"

The group eyed him critically but stayed silent. Thinking he wasn't going to get an answer, he turned to leave. As he was about to take his first step, one of the older members spoke.

"Waall," he said in his Boston accent, "We aim to join the rebel army. We are just waiting for the Captain."

"Captain? What Captain?"

"Captain Wimler, of course. Don't you know nothing?" piped a squirrelly-looking girl with oily hair dropping into her eyes.

"Sorry, I just got here," Mathew said, talking to the older man and purposely ignoring the girl.

"Captain Wimler is the leader of the Free Army. He is looking for volunteers. If he approves us, we will be joining him in his fight against the aliens," he expounded, mightily puffing out his bony chest while scratching his heavily whiskered jowls.

"The Free Army?"

"Yes, that's what the rebel army is calling itself," added a third member of the group. This one was too gaunt to even be described as thin. He wore his clothes like a scarecrow, a walking billboard for how much people had suffered so far under alien rule.

Mathew's heart was beating wildly as he listened to the chaos around him. He didn't know what to do. He was standing in the heart of the rebellion. He swallowed hard as he tried to figure out his next step. Hoping to see this Captain himself, he set off down the crowded road. When he finally came to the end, he was confronted with a cobblestone path leading up a hill. As he started up the slope, he took in his surroundings. The Charlestown Bridge was in the distance, as well as parts of the North End. He saw hundreds of destroyed buildings as well as burnt out vehicles. Destroyed naval ships listed, half sunk in the harbor. Farther out to sea vessels were moving about, but they were too far away to identify. Suddenly, he was gripped by cold panic. Up ahead was an alien hover-craft. Just sitting there? Should he turn around and go back? Should he run? Other people were going about their business, ignoring the alien vehicle. This only confused him more.

Someone spoke from behind. "Don't worry, son, that's been out of commission a while now. A few of the boys took out the alien buggers some nights back. Hell of a fight, but our boys got the jump on them and were successful in eliminating the whole patrol. Too bad we don't know how to start the darn thing. It would be great to use their weapons against them. That thing's got a laser gun strong enough it could bring down a skyscraper in seconds. I'm guarding it till the Captain gets here."

Turning around Mathew noticed a middle-aged man missing a leg. He was leaning against a light pole, holding a sword in his hand and a gun in his belt. He had a black patch over his left eye and a scar down the same cheek. He looked as if he'd just stepped out of a *Pirates of the Caribbean* movie. It would have been funny, if it wasn't for the current situation.

"Thanks for the info," Mathew replied trying to remain calm. "Do you know when the Captain is getting here?"

"Soon," he said, looking up the hill.

In the distance Mathew could hear yelling and cheering. Somebody shouted, "They're coming! The Free Army is coming! They smacked those aliens right in the kisser and walked away to tell the tale," he sang into the air.

For a moment Mathew's knees shook like jello. He had not known what to expect, but it sure wasn't this. All these people were cheering, ready to join the fight. But even with all the excitement in the air, the fear and tension of an upcoming war was rife.

As Mathew debated heading back home, something screeched through the air over his head. Seconds later a large explosion sounded and a building farther up collapsed. Explosion after explosion ripped through the air. Screams of pain and agony resonated. Ugly streams of black smoke arched against the dark blue sky as the alien ships released their missiles. More and more missiles were fired. Buildings were destroyed in seconds; bodies were flung around like rag dolls. Mathew stood frozen in place, not knowing what to do.

"Get down!" screamed the one-legged pirate as he hobbled away.

Reclaiming his wits, Mathew dropped to the ground, covering his head with his hands. The alien forces had turned their guns on Charlestown and the rebel convention. Red-hot missiles and alien projectiles screamed through the air, tearing into anything and everything. Pretty soon nothing and nobody would be left standing. The area was quickly going up in flames. Mathew was trapped.

People were running through the rubble and smoldering buildings. Many were trying to leave the area as they rushed toward the bridge. Everywhere chaos reigned. People screamed and writhed on the ground wounded, limbs missing, their life's blood flowing out. He saw dozens of bodies sprawled out in puddles of blood, buildings demolished, and craters in the ground the size of Olympic size swimming pools. The destruction and devastation was tremendous. What seemed like hours was no more than a few minutes. Mathew lay there trembling, unable to move. The shock of so many bodies in conjunction with the noise, mayhem, and explosions was too much for his mind to process.

"Get out of here!" someone shouted. "It's raining missiles. They mean business this time."

"Disobedience will be punished," blared the alien ships.

Gathering himself, Mathew forced himself through the shock and terror and ran with the others. He had no idea where to run. There was no way he could go back while the bombardment continued. All around him people were running, looking for cover, even going so far as to throw up barricades. For a second Mathew thought about crawling behind one of the barricades and lying flat on the ground. But none of these hastily built shelters looked strong enough to stop a water balloon, let alone alien bullets. Red-hot missiles were streaking overhead. Buildings were collapsing, and rebels were scattering like rats abandoning a sinking ship.

As he ducked behind a smoldering car to catch his breath, he came face to face with two other wannabe rebels who were doing the same. Trying to offer as small as a target as possible, he crouched low to the ground, avoiding the glowing embers scattered about. "How long will this go on?" Mathew shouted.

"Till they run out of bullets or we are all dead, whichever comes first," replied the tall one with the ripped shirt and dirty jeans. "Are you okay?"

"Scared out of my mind, but okay," he panted, trying to get himself into a more comfortable position.

"Well I'd put some pressure on that noggin of yours if I were you, or you'll bleed to death before you do."

Reaching up and feeling his head, he felt wetness. Bringing his hand down he saw blood covering it. He must have been grazed by some sort of projectile and didn't notice a thing in all the bedlam. He could feel the blood dribbling down his shirt, but before he could think about it, he was thrown a dirty towel from one of his recent acquaintances.

"Use this. You'll be okay, head wounds bleed a lot, but it looks like you were just nicked. You'll be fine, but you'll have a huge headache later, that is if you survive."

"Who are you?" asked the short stocky fellow next to him as another missile exploded.

"Name's Mathew, Mathew Holloway."

"I'm Gus and this is Harry," he said pointing to the short stocky guy.

"What regiment you with, Mathew?" asked Gus.

"Regiment? Uuhh, I'm not with a regiment. I just came to see the rebel army."

"Well, get a good gander. Might be the last time you see them," said Harry peeking over the hood of the car. "We have to move, we can't stay here for much longer," he added, nodding at his friend.

"You want to come with us, Mathew?" asked Gus.

Mathew didn't answer. He was staring across the block toward the majority of the destruction. He swore he had just seen his friend Dillon running with a group of soldiers. Did he really see him, or was it the blow to the head that made him think so? And if it was Dillon, what was he doing here? Why was he running toward the alien ships and not away from them? Either way he had to find out if it was his friend, and then figure out what was going on and then decide how to remove them both from this newest pandemonium.

"What you looking at?" inquired Harry. "We're moving out if you want to come." When he didn't get an answer, he turned to his tall friend, adding, "Looks like that blow to the head was stronger than what he originally thought."

"Leave him. He'll just slow us down. Every man for himself, as they say. Let's go!" He yelled, as he unglued himself from the pavement and dodged out from behind the burning vehicle. His girth was definitely deceiving when it came to his speed and agility. Gus raced to catch his friend, avoiding bullets and pieces of falling concrete. They had barely made fifty yards when an alien aircraft buzzed overhead, strafing the street once more. Upon seeing this they both dropped behind a crumbling, bullet painted wall, seeking coverage. Mathew watched as they both rose to their feet making sure the alien fighter had left the area. Bent over, they ran down the street. They made it to the next corner and disappeared into the bellowing smoke.

CHAPTER 5

• • •

INSTEAD OF FOLLOWING THEM, MATHEW turned and ran in the other direction. Heading toward the alien forces and where he had last seen his friend, he came into a group of men piling up a rock wall. Stopping to catch his breath, he waited for someone to confront him. In all the commotion, no one paid him any attention. So he continued his charge across the street. He started up the next sloping avenue, jumping over a broken concrete barrier. All he could see was smoke at the top of the hill. He scrambled upward. Suddenly, a man covered in dirt passed him, going down.

"Any word on reinforcements?" he inquired, looking over Mathew's shoulder.

Red-faced and short of breath, Mathew realized that the man was talking to him. "Don't know!" he answered, trying not to trip over the rubble or his own two feet.

Without slowing his pace, the runner kept going. Reaching the top of the hill, Mathew stopped to catch his breath and survey his surroundings. Down the other side was a large group of armed rebels. They were crouched down in a sort of trench, looking away from him in the opposite direction. Suddenly, he was surprised by a roar of laughter and cheering.

"Look, everyone, reinforcements are here!" someone yelled.

Mathew, his face hot with embarrassment, peered into a sea of grinning faces. He just stood there, not knowing what to do. More laughter swept through the rebel lines as the joke was repeated over and over. People were pointing at him and laughing. Once over his initial shock, Mathew got angry, not realizing that this was more of a release of nervous energy on the part of the rebels, than a jab at him.

Before he could react and make a bigger fool of himself, a hand suddenly gripped him by the shirt and pulled him down behind a barricade. Instinctively throwing his hands up to protect his face and head, Mathew spun around to see who had grabbed him.

"Mathew! What are you doing here! Is that blood? What happened to your head?"

"Dillon!"

Mathew was so happy to see his best friend, he momentarily forgot about the danger they were in. He quickly threw his arms around Dillon and lifted him clear off the ground. He didn't even bother to wonder what anyone would think of his less than masculine reaction.

"Dillon! I saw you running, and I had to find you," he said, releasing his friend, who just stood there looking at him. "What are you doing here? Are you crazy? We should get out of here and go home. Your parents would crucify you if they knew you were here. Don't you know there's a battle going on?" Mathew was so nervous and excited about finding his friend; he couldn't get the words out fast enough.

"Slow down, buddy. Take a deep breath. We can't go anywhere. LOOK! " He said turning his friend around.

Spying through a hole in the barricade, Mathew gulped with fear. He pulled back from the hole, awestruck by the sight below him. A horde of aliens was heading their way! He had never seen so many together at one time. They kept pouring out of their ships, like water from a busted damn. They were loaded with automatic weapons, hand-guns, grenades, and all types of alien armament. There were plasma guns the size of bazookas and rocket launchers in the hundreds. He saw hover crafts in the shape of snow-mobiles with two riders sitting back to back, one operating the controls the other aiming and controlling a laser weapon attached to the rear frame. These machines floated propelled by rockets and were able to provide cover as the alien troops advanced on the rebel forces. The alien soldiers lined up in formation as they marched in their direction.

Weapons and body armor flashed in the noon sun. The alien leaders, uniforms gleaming, stood out in front, weapons pointing at the rebel forces. Signaling the hover-crafts to take their positions, they began their attack.

Mathew pulled away from his hole. Wiping sweat from his eyes, his head throbbing like a bass drum, he uttered his first prayer in months. He thought of his mother and how she would handle his death and felt bad for the sorrow he was about to cause her. He estimated his chances at a trillion to one that he would survive the next hour. Dillon head bowed was making his own peace with the big guy in the sky. At least the two would die with his best friend at his side.

"Here they come!" someone shouted.

Thump-thump, thump-thump, their boots sounded in the air. Click-clack, click-clack, their weapons resonated against their armor. Explosions sounded as the hovercrafts delivered their deadly payloads. Yells and screams could be heard farther down the line. Many if not all the rebels would lose their lives today. They'd leave behind families and friends, but their ideals and sacrifice would stand true and solid in their loved one's memories. Was pessimism the byproduct of war or the crutch that plagued the battle? Would they hold it together or fold like a house of cards at the end? Mathew thought of his dead father and the service he had given to his country. Deep down Mathew knew he would stand tall and proud, bravely giving his life.

"Hold your fire, men. Nobody shoots till I give the word," shouted a grizzled older man, who seemed to be in command. He was wearing an old Rolling Stones tee-shirt and a Boston Red Sox cap. Holding an automatic weapon, with a berretta pistol in his holster, he marched up and down the line, giving orders and whispering encouragement. He was flanked by two men who looked to be twins from different mothers. Both stood tall and straight, one dark haired, the other blond. With solemn faces they followed on the heels of their leader, each holding a rocket launcher as if it were an extension of their body. These men reminded Mathew of his father, they were true soldiers, born and bred for battle, protecting the constitution.

Mathew's father was a member of the navy SEALS, a Special Forces group tasked with the most important, most dangerous missions. These men with their close-cropped hair and severe looks were probably the same. At any other time Mathew would have approached them and asked them outright if they belonged to the elite fighting unit. Proudly, he would tell them he was the son of a former Special Forces team member, but this was neither the time nor the place for childish behavior.

Dillon was shaking beside Mathew. Whether it nerves or excitement, Mathew couldn't tell. He held an old rifle, its muzzle pointing toward the incoming aliens. His own teeth chattering, his knees shaking Mathew glanced at his best friend. Dillon was the first boy Mathew had met when he moved into the North End.

While his folks were busy supervising the unloading their furniture by the movers, Mathew had explored his new neighborhood. Eventually he found his way to the basketball courts and playground on Prince Street. A small park in the middle of the Italian district, it offered shade and entertainment. Large trees and grass dotted the park side of the street, and large brick apartment buildings made up the other side. As he neared the park he saw a woman selling ice cream and cold drinks from a push cart. Suddenly craving an ice cream, he sidled up to the cart, gazed at the picture display on the side, and tried to decide what flavor he wanted.

"Try the lemon ice, my favorite," said a voice behind him. Turning around, Mathew found himself staring into the eyes of a boy his age. Four and a half feet tall, with blond hair and blue eyes, he was wearing black basketball shorts, a yellow Pokemon tee shirt, and red Pump Nikes. "Hi, my name is Dillon," he said, sticking his hand out for a shake. "You must be new around here."

"Hi, I'm Mathew. How'd you know I'm new?"

Laughing he said, "I grew up around here so I know just about everyone, but the thing that said 'newbie' was the fact that you were staring at the display. Everybody around here knows that Mrs. Mary has the best frozen ice in the neighborhood, and they hardly ever order anything else. It's cool, it's fresh, and more importantly it's only fifty cents. You're not rich, are you, 'cause if you are, forget what I said."

"No, I'm not rich," Mathew replied, his mouth watering with anticipation. His parents had always taught him to be polite and friendly, so he asked Dillon if he could treat him to some frozen ice to repay the lesson. "How about I buy us both one and you can tell me about the neighborhood? We just moved here today, and I don't know much about this place."

"For Mrs. Mary's frozen ice, I'll not only give you the scoop about your new hood, but I'll also show you around and introduce you to everyone. Mrs. Mary, two of your lemon ices please. My good friend Mathew…"

"Holloway," Mathew said quickly, reaching into his pocket for his money.

"Holloway is paying," Dillon finished.

From that day forward they were inseparable, spending all their free time together. They went to the same school, sat next to each other in class, played on the same team in little league; they took karate classes together, moving quickly through the ranks and earning their black belts at the same time, and they got into all kinds of scrapes and mischief. They spent so much time in each other's homes that it was inevitable that their parents would become great friends. The boys especially enjoyed their hiking and camping trips and all the nature and survival training they got from Mathew's dad.

Now, his friend was urging him, "Leave, Mathew! Run, get away! They'll overrun us in a minute."

"I can't," cried Mathew. "I won't leave without you. Come with me!"

"I'm a rebel fighter now," Dillon said looking around wildly. "My brother is here. He'll take care of me. Just go!"

"Dillon! Pay attention. Look to your position or we'll all be killed," yelled the grizzled-chinned officer. "It's too late for anyone to leave now. The first wave is almost on top of us."

"Yes, Sir! Captain Wimler, Sir!" yelled Dillon.

So this was Captain Wimler. He definitely acted the hard-ass even with that Rolling Stones tee shirt. But for some reason Mathew had pictured him to be a lot taller.

"It's party time, folks. Everyone pick a "partner" and get ready to dance," the Captain shouted as he went back and forth, his shadows following closely behind.

Hearing this, Mathew felt his knees suddenly buckle. He sank to the ground, leaning against the barricade. What had he gotten himself into? He locked his eyes on the opening. He saw the aliens advance. They scrambled over the barriers placed by the rebels, pausing every so often to straighten their lines.

Here they came again, straight for them. Mathew felt sick. It was like a bad dream. He began to pick out details and differences in the alien forces' armaments. Some he had seen on the streets of Boston. Others were new to him. Some were ordinary alien soldiers, others elite Magar combat troops. Bulletproof leathers were the fashion of the day. Helmets with built in com units covered sloping foreheads and lathering mouths. Body armor shielded torsos and arms. They all wore skin tight gloves over their claw-like fingers to help grip their weapons. Heavy military boots and rough trousers with utility belts full of weapons and God knew what else completed the ensemble. If not for the gravity of the situation Mathew would have expected to see a famous director in the background directing the action, the drama unfolding resembling the opening scene of a high budget sci-fi movie.

What was everyone waiting for? Why didn't someone give the order to fire? Were they waiting for the aliens to reach the rebel lines so as to invite them over for milk and cookies? Was everyone too shocked to move? Why was everyone so quiet?

Mathew was mesmerized by the silence. Nobody moved. Nobody breathed. The first wave of aliens was less than fifteen yards away and getting closer by the second. Crossing himself, he thought of Father James and all the Sunday school lessons he and Dillon had struggled through. He now prayed that God chose that minute to help the needy and confirm his compassion and benevolence.

"Forgive me, Father, for I have sinned…,"

"Fire! Aim for their legs and don't miss…!!!"

"Their legs are their weak spot," breathed Dillon right before he discharged his weapon.

The blast was deafening. Hundreds of weapons of all sizes and makes fired at the same time. Mathew couldn't see anything through the smoke. He felt as if he were swimming under water. He couldn't hear anything. Then came the screaming and rasping anguish of the wounded. Through the hole, he saw that the alien force was no longer advancing. That first volley must have been quite a shock. Hundreds of aliens were down. Some dead, some dying, others severely wounded.

"Hold your fire! Hold your fire," someone screamed over and over.

No one made a sound. Even the rebels were awed by the destruction of their initial volley. They stared at the alien bodies littering the street. Several rebels threw-up. Others just gaped, not knowing what to do next.

"Reload! Reload," echoed throughout the ranks.

Mathew craned his neck, trying to see who was yelling. It was the Captain. He was alone, his shadows either occupied or dead. He was standing hatless behind the firing line of the rebels. Even as Mathew spotted him, a single shot rang out from the direction of the alien forces. He saw the Captain spin in place like a child's top; his head was no longer part of his body. Then he crumbled. Mathew couldn't believe it. Their leader dead, killed by a single bullet. If he wasn't scared stiff, he'd throw up the contents of his stomach. The spray of blood and brains pelted several rebels who weren't as stoic as Mathew, adding the contents of their stomachs to the red and gray matter already covering the ground. This set off a chain reaction as more and more rebels joined in the emetic projectile event. Nothing like a contagious round of vomiting to put things in perspective.

Now a second wave of aliens was charging up the hill. Totally disregarding their fallen comrades, they marched over their sprawled bodies. Dillon was next to him, reloading his weapon. He was pulling bullets out of his pockets and loading his rifle with trembling hands. All up and down the rebel line, men were hastily reloading, as they wiped the vomit from their lips and spit out bile.

"Fire!" someone yelled. The chain of command already reestablished, the deceased Captain taking his place among other fallen leaders. The front lines of battle were hard fought by leveraging lives and limbs. And even though others stepped forward to take command and soldiers picked up dropped weapons to take up the battle, the dead were mourned.

Mathew spied through his hole as the rebels fired. More aliens crumbled to the ground. The noise was unbearable. The yelling of the rebel forces, the firing of weapons, the screaming of the wounded, now on both sides, was enough to drive anyone insane. Grown men cried like children, begging for their mothers. Aliens howled in a foreign tongue, weapons discharging. Orders screamed on both sides contributed to the bedlam and pandemonium, causing sane men to lose their minds.

The second rebel volley was just as deadly. The pounding of hundreds of boots told him the aliens were still coming. Weapons continued to fire on the rebel side as more and more aliens advanced. Although the rebels were now taking significant casualties themselves, they continued to persevere. As they aimed and fired low into the legs of the enemy, they created both wounded as well as chaos for the alien force. As more and more aliens fell, it was becoming more difficult for the enemy troops to advance over the bodies of their fellow soldiers. The ragtag lot of rebels with their sheer will and limited firepower had torn to shreds the charging extraterrestrials. Mathew couldn't believe his eyes. The Magar forces were retreating!

No one celebrated behind the barricade. Nobody was talking. Most sat with lost faces, trying to catch their breaths and make sense of what had just happened. Others uttered prayers or just cried into their dirty sleeves, mourning the dead or grieving for their own doomed lives Mathew didn't know. He was in just as much shock as anyone around him. Dillon was just staring in front of him, nervously biting his cheek, tears running down his face. Mathew crouched beside him. Some of the rebels were already reloading; others were helping the wounded or removing the dead away from the barricade.

It felt as if time had stopped. Minutes turned to hours. Everyone was exhausted. But Mathew noted the alien troops regrouping. They were tending to their own wounded and dead. Their hovercrafts long destroyed, posed no threat to the rebel forces. Not only could they not indiscriminately fire on them, but they also couldn't glean any information spying from above. Having lost most of their commanding officers in the first two attacks, the aliens seemed unsure on how to proceed. You had to give them credit. Unlike many of our previous American military commanders sitting in situation rooms behind the line, there was no one leading from behind for these guys. They wanted to be in the heat of the battle, alongside their troops, no matter what the consequences. The problem was it was only a matter of time before reinforcements were called in and new leaders installed ,to take command and continue the battle.

"Will they come back?" someone asked.

"More than likely. They're reforming already," someone answered.

"Wish I had a gun," Mathew said enviously, eyeing his friend's weapon.

Dillon asked, "I didn't know you knew how to use one?"

"I don't know how to use the one you're holding but my dad taught me the basics. I could help if I had a weapon. I've been watching you and you couldn't hit the side of a barn if it ran up and fell on you," he said hoping to lighten the mood.

Someone must have heard Mathew because in the next second he was holding a weapon.

"Fellow down the line got himself killed. He won't be needing his anymore. It's an AK47, one of the best automatic weapons ever made. Just point and shoot. It's got a full clip, and here's some extra ammo. Just keep your head down," he said throwing Mathew a cloth sack filled with ammunition clips.

"Thanks, mister."

"Don't mention it, kid. I don't think I'm doing you any favors, but we can use all the help we can get. Especially, since our friend Dillon here couldn't shoot himself out of a paper bag," he added with a wink. With those final words he moved off down the line.

"Who was that?" Mathew asked his friend as soon as the man was out of range.

"Beats me. Just don't get killed. I don't need your mom pissed at me. I've got enough problems." Watching Mathew fiddle with his newly acquired weapon he jokingly added, "Figuring out what end to point at the enemy and what end to put against my shoulder."

"Uh...duh...is this where the bullets go?" Mathew quipped, doing his best impression of the Neanderthal in his favorite movie, *Encino Man*.

"Oh, and by the way, welcome to the rebel army," Dillon said with a smirk.

• • •

HOLDING HIS GUN TIGHTLY MATHEW turned his attention back to the alien forces. He crouched low into a more comfortable position. Going over his weapon, trying to remember what his father had told him and what he had seen other soldiers do during his excursions to the rebel camp, he once again questioned his courage. Would he be able to fire on the alien forces or would he wet his pants when they got near? It was one thing watching others fire their weapons and another to stare down the barrel of your own gun, firing at an advancing enemy force and hoping and praying no one shot back at you. He didn't think he would feel any remorse for killing these aliens, not after what they had done to his country and his world. They had killed so many people the numbers of the dead had to be in the billions, judging by what they had done in his country alone. They had killed his father, his friends, relatives and neighbors. They deserved to pay for what they'd done. With that final thought, his resolve was set. He would fight to the end, exacting payback for all the senseless deaths and devastation they caused. He would do his best to punish the Magars for what they had done.

"Do you know what to do?" asked Dillon with concern.

"Yeah, I'm good. We've played so much *Halo,* I should be a pro," Mathew answered, trying to hide how scared he really was. "Wish we had something to drink, I'm dying of thirst." As the minutes ticked away, Mathew settled down. His hands stopped shaking, and he didn't feel like throwing up. Well almost. He was just about to doze off, when all of a sudden there was a shout to arms.

"Get ready! Here they come again!"

A cold pain seared through his belly, his muscles tensing up all over again. Wiping the sweat from his eyes with the back of his hand, he tried to calm his breathing and focus. He focused his aim by sighting along the barrel, like his father had taught him. He waited for the order to fire.

"Don't forget to hold the butt to your shoulder tightly. If you don't it'll kick back harder than a mule and knock you backwards," Dillon said as he kept his eyes on the enemy.

Mathew laughed nervously, as he repositioned his weapon more snuggly against his shoulder. The Magars were picking their way through the carnage. Moving slower this time, they appeared even more menacing than before. They kept in formation. Closer and closer they advanced. Mathew concentrated on his target, an especially large alien in full gear. He held his aim below the waist, waiting for the order to fire.

"Fire!"

Mathew pulled the trigger a split second later. It seemed as if once the weapon started firing it kept firing forever. He wondered when it would stop. Then he suddenly remembered to take his hand off the trigger. His ears were ringing and his shoulder was numb from the weapon's recoil. Looking through his makeshift window he saw several dead or wounded aliens in his vicinity. It was a chilling sight, blood, gore, and limbs scattered about. A few errant shots could still be heard in the distance amongst the screams of pain.

Amid the cries of agony, Mathew thought he heard cheers. Wondering if he was losing his mind, he looked around him. All he could see was smoke and dust swirling in the air, clouding his field of vision. As the air cleared, he saw that once again they had been successful. Alien bodies were piled up waist high, especially close to their barricade. An occasional shot rang out from both sides. Keeping his head down, he tried to assess the situation.

Next to him Dillon sat with a bewildered look. "Is that cheering I hear?"

Before Mathew could answer, someone yelled, "We did it! They're retreating. We beat them back again!"

"Yeah, but they'll return," Dillon muttered looking dejected, "If we don't get some more ammunition soon, we're done for. I'm down to my last ten bullets," he said reloading his rifle.

"What'd you mean?" asked Mathew. With his adrenaline pumping and the ringing in his ears from the noise and the blow to the head he'd received earlier, Mathew wasn't sure if he'd heard his friend correctly.

"Bullets, Mathew! Bullets. We are running out of bullets. Remember some of these weapons haven't been fired in decades. It's hard to find bullets for all these different guns, especially since the Magars went on their destroy the human's weapons campaign," Dillon said sarcastically.

Before Mathew could say anything, his friend apologized. "Sorry, Mathew, that was uncalled for. I'm just nervous and scared. My brother tells me of all the problems the rebel forces are facing. Lack of proper weapons and ammunition is one of the worst."

"There's no more bullets anywhere?" exclaimed Mathew, still not grasping the reality.

"If there is, nobody's told me. The last I heard, they had sent out people to collect all they could find for the rebel army. That's why they raided the alien compound last night. They were hoping to find weapons and ammunition. All they found was some alien laser rifles that they haven't figured out how to work yet. The one positive was that they destroyed one of the alien ships with some old semtex someone had been hoarding. This not only got the alien's attention but also managed to royally piss them off, so much so that it seems they've sent half their forces at us."

Mathew glanced around, hoping to find a solution. He noticed discarded weapons all over. Some were piled in stacks. Others were thrown haphazardly to the ground.

Noticing a rocket launcher lying nearby, he asked, "Why hasn't anyone fired that thing?"

"Someone either forgot we had it or there's no ammunition. My money's on no ammo."

Mathews' elation over their recent success evaporated. He didn't see any enemy troops but knew they were out there. His fellow rebels were shouting for ammunition and no one said they had extra to share.

"Maybe the aliens have had enough," he said unconvincingly, more to placate his own fears.

It didn't take long to get his answer. The thumping of boots and the clatter of weapons and armor warned him that the aliens were returning. As the afternoon wore on, they waited patiently for the enemy to engage. Suddenly, out of the growing shadows, the aliens advanced.

A voice growled, "Make every shot count. Wait until they get close and make every shot count."

Closer and closer they came. Their armor was now dirty and bloody. This only made them more ominous and intimidating. You didn't have to speak their language to know that their leaders were ordering their troops forward. This wasn't some sort of skirmish against a few disorganized rebels. This was brutal and savage war. Winner takes all; loser dies.

As the aliens came closer to the barricade, the rebels took their time to aim before firing. Mathew leveled his weapon and squeezed the trigger. Both his own and Dillon's shots rang simultaneously. Other shots rang out behind him. Though aliens fell, others kept steadily advancing. Out of the corner of his eye, he saw a rebel break out and run away. More followed.

"Let's go, Mathew! Come on! We have to go. I'm out of bullets," yelled Dillon, urging him away from the barricade.

"I still have some left. I can take some more aliens down. You go," Mathew yelled, not even bothering to turn around. Caught up in the moment, his attention captive, his focus laser sharp, he waited like an alcoholic at a bar for a free drink.

Dillon reached down and grabbed Mathew's shoulder. He was in a crouch, trying to avoid the flying debris from all the alien bullets and blasts that were now pummeling their position. "Mathew, listen. Please."

Mathew heard screams of retreat. "REBELS, RETREAT NOW!"

Then he saw the aliens swarm over the barricade. Confusion reigned. Screams, curses, and shouts added to the confusion and chaos. Some rebels were engaging the enemy in hand to hand combat. Some used their useless weapons as clubs. Others threw fists with bare hands. In all the commotion Mathew heard bones snap as they made contact with reinforced armor or solid helmets. Unable to fire his weapon out of fear of hitting his own people, he sat hopeless watching the unfolding melee. Dillon's urging continued, forcing Mathew out of his stupor. Standing up, he was about to follow his friend when he felt a massive blow on his upper arm. He fell back landing against the barricade wall. Why was his vision blurry? He must have sand in my eyes, he thought. Why couldn't he raise his arm to wipe his eyes? And why did Dillon have to keep yelling in his ear?

"Mathew! Mathew! You're hit!! Stay down," Dillon screamed.

Mathew felt himself lifted off the ground and fly into the air. He was weightless, a feather, a gliding bird. He was floating in a cloud. He was soaring through the sky. Then all of a sudden, blackness enveloped him, as he crashed to the ground.

• • •

CHAPTER 7

WHEN MATHEW FINALLY WOKE UP, he couldn't fathom where he was. He knew it was nighttime because he was staring right at the bright moon in the dark night. He saw a few twinkling lights flashing farther up in space, but mostly he saw stars. Both, celestial bodies and stars of pain. His body was racked by a searing hot pain radiating down his right side. Squeezing his eyes shut and taking some deep breaths, he tried to get control of himself. With tears of pain running down his face, he realized that he was in a moving vehicle. He was brought fully awake, as the vehicle hit a pothole. He closed his eyes and tried not to cry out but a small whimper escaped. He moaned even louder a few seconds later, when the truck hit another crater jarring him down to his bones. Gritting his teeth so he wouldn't swear out loud, he tried to maneuver into a more comfortable position.

"Are you awake? How are you feeling?"

Mathew opened his eyes and found Dillon staring down at him. Where'd he come from? What were they doing here? Weren't they supposed to be in bed, tomorrow a school day? These thoughts and others plagued his disoriented mind as his body was jostled. He was so nauseous, he was sure he was going to throw up all over himself if the turbulent shaking didn't stop. It felt worse than last year when he had gone on the Cyclone ride at Six Flags, after eating three chili cheese hot dogs and a supreme nachos with extra guacamole and sour cream, and washing the whole thing down with a 32oz. Mountain Dew slurpee. He had thought that was the worst day of his life, but that was a walk in the park, compared with what he was going through now.

"You had me worried there for a second. You'll be fine, dude, don't worry. Just hang on. We're almost there," Dillon said, his voice faltering with concern.

Mathew didn't care. All he wanted was to go back to sleep and get away from the pain. His shoulder was on fire. He could feel his aching body covered in bruises every time the driver hit a bump. He must have passed out again, because the next thing he remembered was someone yelling orders and men cursing and somewhere in the distance, the discharging of automatic weapons.

Where was he? What was going on? Slowly as the cob webs started to clear, he remembered the rebels' battle with the aliens. Taking a deep breath, he gently raised his head and looked around. Figures were moving in the darkness. He saw parked vehicles, equipment and bodies littering the ground. He realized he himself was stretched out on the ground, his head resting on someone's smelly sweatshirt.

The air was filled with moans of suffering and pain. Multiple cries of pain, coming from many different directions, made him realize that there were many wounded. He didn't see anyone around him to ask for help, so he tried to get up on his own. His head spun dizzily but he was able to stand. His shoulder throbbed but slowly his head cleared. Cautiously he took a step forward and was happy to find himself moving, although he was stiff and sore. Someone had bandaged his shoulder and his arm was in a sling. Although it still hurt, the pain was manageable. They'd probably given him medicine for the pain while he was asleep. Other than some cuts and bruises and a huge knot on his head he felt okay.

"Hey, it's about time you got up. How are you feeling?" Dillon asked as he came up on the run. Behind him followed an older man wearing glasses and sporting a stethoscope. His sleeves were rolled up to his elbows and he was holding a gym bag. "This is Doc Stevens. He patched you up."

"Hello, son. Glad to see you're up. You had a hell of a time, getting shot through the shoulder and a possible concussion from whatever grazed you, all in the same day. Now, sit still while I examine you." After a cursory examination, during which Mathew was asked how he felt and if he was seeing double, the doctor poked and prodded his shoulder, eliciting several cries in response.

Once the doctor had checked him over, he was released into the care of his friend. "You'll be fine," the doctor said. "Just take it easy for a while and make sure to change the bandages every couple of days. The bullet went through your shoulder and came out your bicep. You were lucky. It didn't hit any bone. You will be sore for a while but should heal fully, if it doesn't get infected. I told your friend Dillon how to clean it. Now I have to go. Some of the others weren't so lucky. Oh, I gave you something for the pain, so you might feel a little lightheaded. It should pass in a couple of hours. If the pain is too much to bear, come find me and I'll give you something to help take the edge off."

"Thanks, Doc," Mathew mumbled feeling guilty. He was happy to be alive and not seriously injured but he was sad for the rebels who'd died. How many husbands, fathers, brothers, and sisters weren't ever going home again? How much sadness and grief did the human race still have to suffer?

He heard Dillon laugh as the doctor said something as he was leaving. Turning toward him he said, "Dude, thought you were a goner there for a second!"

"Got lucky, but if I don't get something to drink, I think I will die. It feels as if someone started a fire in my throat."

"Can you walk?"

"If I say no, will you carry me?"

Dillon answered, "Only as far as I can throw you. Seriously, are you okay? You really had me worried."

"Yeah, I'm okay. And thanks. What time is it?"

"It's about three in the morning. Okay, let's go. Follow me. They have some food, supplies, and water around the back of that truck in the middle of the yard."

Looking around, Mathew realized they were in some sort of compound. He could make out more details, now that his eyes were adjusting to the darkness. People were moving amidst scattered tents and supplies. He was surprised at all the activity this time of night.

With Dillon supporting him, they made their way toward the supplies. Once there, he downed three bottles of lukewarm water and a very stale protein bar. He wasn't about to complain. He was famished, and it revived him.

"What happened, Dillon?" he asked his friend, who was gnawing on a moldy bar.

"It was awful! After you got shot and fell down, you whacked your head on a rock and passed out. The aliens broke through our barricade and swarmed all over us. Everyone wanted to fight it out, but our leaders yelled for us to retreat. A good thing, too. When you went down, I wanted to get you away but didn't know how. When the retreat was called, our people started to back away, carrying wounded with them. One of the men down the line ran over to help me. Together, we got you to one of the trucks they were using to cart off the wounded. I guess we were lucky to get away alive," he finished. Finally frustrated with the protein bar he was chewing, he spit the whole mouthful to the ground and threw the rest of it across the compound in disgust. "That sucked," he said, drinking from a bottle of water, probably trying to wash away the lingering moldy taste in his mouth.

"Thanks, man, I owe you a big one," Mathew said with tears of gratitude. "If you weren't there, I'd be a goner. "I don't even remember getting hit. All I remember was the aliens breaking through the barricade and you yelling in my ear. You were so annoying that you reminded me of Mrs. Reynolds, our old science teacher. Remember her? That woman could talk your ear off and still say nothing interesting."

"Don't mention it. You would have done the same for me," Dillon replied, turning away, making believe he didn't see Mathew's tears. "Plus, I thought you had a crush on Mrs. Reynolds. You used to make those googly eyes at her all the time in class," he said over his shoulder.

"Googly eyes? Are you crazy? She was older than George Washington and she smelled funny, like moth balls and vapor rub. I wasn't making googly eyes at her. I was trying to stay awake," he said sounding insulted.

Looking off into to the distance, Dillon waited for his friend to compose himself. He'd been through enough, and he didn't want him to feel embarrassed for crying. To be honest, Mathew was dealing with the whole situation better than he would have. If he had been the one shot, he'd be crying like a little baby with a full diaper from a case of the creamed spinach runs. Getting shot must hurt like hell. He had heard grown men sob like little children. Turning back to his friend, he found him lost in his own thoughts.

Mathew thought of all the dead and injured and said nothing. He was upset and angry at the situation. He was wondering what his mom and Molly must be thinking at home. He'd never stayed out this late before. His mother would be frantic, assuming the worst. If only there were some way to notify her he was okay. "I have to let my mom know I'm okay. She is probably worried sick," he said suddenly, coming out of his mental funk.

"I was thinking the same thing. My parents know that my brother was involved with the resistance but they don't know about me. They're going to kill me when I get back. The problem is we can't go back now. The aliens are on watch everywhere. Nothing and nobody is getting by them. But you're right; we have to let them know we're alive and well. I'm sure they're going to crucify us themselves once they learn what we've been doing, but we can worry about that later."

Suddenly Mathew felt extremely tired, and his shoulder was throbbing. "I'm feeling tired. I--I better lie down again and get some rest."

Dillon led him toward the barracks, where he found an empty bunk. He was out cold in no time, his weary body craving sleep.

CHAPTER 8

• • •

MATHEW RESTED FOR THE NEXT several days. He spent
most of his time either in his bunk or exploring the rebel
compound. It was located in some sort of canyon, probably in the northern part of the state. The day before he
had ventured up one of the canyon walls to get a better
view of his temporary home. He had climbed about a
hundred feet using tree branches and roots to pull himself
up the steep embankment, careful not to further irritate
his already injured shoulder. With his back against a tree,
he surveyed the camp. It was laid out in a large rectangle.
The command tent was situated toward the rear corner,
next to the munitions and armament tent. The motor
pool was in the middle, with the mess tent in the corner
opposite the command center. The mess hall, made up of
multiple lean-tos and scattered rough wooden tables, was
in the lower left hand corner. The rest of camp was filled
with small- and medium-size personal tents. There was
only one road leading in and out of camp. Farther down
the road he noticed a fire tower served as a lookout post.

His wounds were minor compared to some of the other injured rebels. Though he experienced a small fever and isolated bouts of pain, his discomfort was temporary. He would heal fully with no ill side effects. The majority of his problems were based on his anxiety and turmoil. What must his mom be going through, wondering where he was? He felt horrible putting his mother through this agony, especially after losing his dad.

On the fifth day, Mathew woke up feeling much better. His shoulder was healing well and he felt well rested. He immediately sought out Dillon, hoping to discuss how to get word to his mother.

Before he even brought up the topic, Dillon said, "I sent a message to my parents and your mom, telling them we were all right. I left out most of the details but mentioned the battle and how we got caught up in it, as innocent bystanders of course. I told them we would go back when things calmed down. The Magars are really having a cow. They've increased patrols exponentially and our scouts tell us they are going crazy trying to find us. They are harassing everyone trying to get information on our whereabouts."

"How did you send a message?" Mathew asked, knowing that all communications media was inoperable.

"One of our scouts, who happens to be a good friend of my father's, was heading in the direction of our homes and he said he would deliver my message without any difficulty." He added, "Don't worry. Because he's old, the aliens don't pay too much attention to him. Little do they know, he's a real devil--one of the best soldiers the rebel army has," he said with a sardonic grin. "My brother has told me some of the stuff the guy's done. He makes James Bond look like a girl scout."

Mathew smiled, thinking of old Mr. Marks. These old guys sure get around, he thought to himself. I guess all that talk about them being the best generation wasn't an exaggeration after all. Goes to show you that experience and good old know-how has its merits.

"Let's get some food. I'm starving," Dillon said heading off toward the mess tent. "I'll share the latest rumors with you over breakfast."

On the walk over, Dillon filled him in on the latest news. The rebel troops were waiting for a new commander to show up and take charge. He was rumored to be an ex-military man who had served in Iran and Afghanistan with our Special Forces teams. He was greatly respected by the powers that be and came highly recommended.

"Mathew they're saying the president himself is sending him!" Dillon exclaimed. "Once the commander organizes things we're going to show these aliens what happens when you mess with us. They say the guy has both the Medal of Honor and the Purple Heart. He spent time undercover, mixing it up with al-Qaeda and ISIS terrorists in the hottest deserts of the Middle East. They're saying he saved a whole army regiment from ambush, in Fallujah, during the battle of Al-Fajr."

"Al-Fajr? My dad told us about it during a camping trip."

While Dillon went to get their food, Mathew tried to recollect his father's tales. Fallujah was a large town forty or so miles west of Baghdad. The Battle of Fallujah was code-named Operation *Al-Fajr*. It was a joint American, Iraqi, and British offensive in December 2004, and was considered the highest point of conflict in Fallujah during the Iraq War. It was led by the US Marine Corps against the Iraqi insurgency stronghold in the city of Fallujah. The US military called it "some of the heaviest urban combat the United States Marines have been involved in since Vietnam." His father's team was providing support and backup, and had firsthand knowledge of the battle.

They were so outnumbered; they didn't think they'd make it out alive. Mathew was surprised to find the similarities to the battle they had just gone through. Before he could think further on the subject, his stomach growled as loudly as a rabid dog. He didn't realize how famished he was, till Dillon got back with two plates loaded with food.

While eating, Mathew heard men grumbling wondering who this new guy was and how much real war experience he had. He heard some say the guy was just a supply sergeant who had never seen any action. Others said he was a wet behind the ears lieutenant who soiled himself every time he heard a gun go off. Those guys in Washington didn't know what they were doing. If they had a clue we wouldn't be in this predicament now. The grumbling and whining continued and Mathew couldn't finish eating his food fast enough ,so he could leave and give his ears a break.

Outside, the camp was bustling. No matter his qualifications, the new commander was highly anticipated. One of the scouts, who had just returned from patrol, reported seeing the new commander and his cavalcade approaching. "There are several Humvees and trucks. I think I even saw a tank or two. He must be bringing supplies with him. Lord knows we can use them. Pretty soon, all we'll be shooting at these aliens with are spitballs. And by the looks of some of you, we're running low on spit," he added, eyeing a group of disheveled rebels standing around doing nothing.

After his little speech, everyone went their own way. Some headed toward the perimeter hoping to catch a glimpse of the convoy. Mathew and Dillon strolled toward a high spot in the compound hoping to spot it too.

The sight of so many down-trodden rebels depressed Mathew. Some were gathering their belongings; others were just lying around. One skinny guy was trying to clean some rust off an old revolver that looked like it belonged to his great-grandfather. Several other groups were busy getting drunk making fools of themselves, acting out some imaginary alien confrontation in which they kicked butt and took names. If they spent more time training and less time play acting, they'd stand a far better chance of surviving a real alien encounter.

"They're a disgrace!" Mathew fumed. "I hope they get punished when the new commander takes over. Why are they even here if they won't take this seriously? They get drunk and make a nuisance of themselves. Their actions disrespect the dead and wounded. They should be ashamed of themselves."

"Relax, Mathew. These guys are here to fight. Others just stay home, waiting for other people to do the dirty work. They probably lost friends and neighbors, and this is the way they cope. We might not agree with their actions, but you have to admit, at least they're here."

Mathew wasn't satisfied. He had a bad feeling that these guys would fight only if they were in the right mood and with the odds fully in their favor. What would happen if they were seriously outnumbered and in dire danger? Would they fight or would they run away? He also wondered if they would follow someone else's orders. Would they stick around, if they didn't like the new leader or his ideas? Or would they sulk away, tail between their legs, complaining that the new guy didn't know anything about war and military protocol? Mathew secretly hoped that there wouldn't come a time when his life depended on them doing the right thing.

A commotion broke out close to the perimeter. Rebels started running in that direction, pushing one another, maneuvering for a better position. The shoving and jostling became so intense that some rebels started to argue amongst themselves, even going so far as to throw punches. Tempers were running thin, the rough conditions and inactivity taking its toll. If ever a leader was needed, the time was now.

"Come on! I think they're here," Dillon shouted, running toward the crowd, avoiding several groups of fighting men and women.

As they reached the perimeter, Mathew could see a plume of dust rising along road. The first vehicle in the convoy came around a corner. Mathew climbed a small wall and saw a man standing on top of a tank, looking around him. As their eyes met, Mathew felt a tremendous relief. The man had to be the commander everyone was talking about. His gaze was ice-cold steel, and even at this distance, he radiated raw power and authority.

He was a big man with a pockmarked face only a mother would call handsome. He had black hair cut short to his scalp. Thick bushy eyebrows shaded eyes so dark that his iris and pupil looked like one. A strong aquiline nose that had seen better days dominated the center of his face, riding rough shod over a severe unsmiling mouth. He had a scar under his left eye extending to his chin, probably compliments of some Afghan fighter. He seemed to be looking through Mathew and taking in the compound and the gathered soldiers at the same time and, in one glance, found them all lacking. A sad look lurked behind his eyes, as if he could tell the future and wasn't happy.

Suddenly cheers broke out. The new commander saluted as he entered the compound. Without saying a word, he jumped off the tank as it came to a stop and headed in the direction of the headquarters. A good hundred yards away, headquarters was a large brown and green military camouflage tent with a painted board with the letters HQ spray painted in white and stuck in the ground in front of the door. Setting a quick pace, he covered the distance in no time, while ignoring the questions hurled at him from all directions. When he reached the door, he turned around and regarded at the assembly one final time before entering HQ.

"Did you see him, Mathew?" asked Dillon. "Did you see his scar? I bet he didn't get that moving supplies around!"

Mathew shook his head. "He definitely looks tough. A bit mysterious even. I wonder if the rebels will follow him. He seems like a no nonsense kind of guy. I don't know how well he and most of these ragtag bunch of wannabe freedom fighters will get along."

• • •

CHAPTER 9

THE DAYS TURNED INTO WEEKS. Mathew and Dillon had heard from their parents and were surprised when they were told to stay put. Conditions at home had deteriorated. The aliens were arresting and detaining all young men and women, still trying to find the people responsible for the assault on the alien compound and for the *Battle of Charlestown*, as it was now being called. They harassed people on the street and broke into people's homes day and night. People were scared and frustrated. Many had been arrested or outright killed for resisting or sassing the alien forces. Punishment was metered out to set examples and promote obedience and subjugation. Mathew and Dillon's families were doing well, spending time together, and generally avoiding contact with the aliens whenever possible. Dillon's brother had returned home after the Battle of Charlestown and was lying low for the time being. To the chagrin of his parents, he was itching to get back to his regiment but had to wait since his unit was temporarily dismantled until things cooled down.

During the hot days that followed, the rebels became an army under the command of Colonel Jason Thomas. They were separated into units and ran drills and different scenarios every day. As was assumed, the Colonel had shown up with all kinds of supplies and weapons. Scouts were sent out on patrols and missions daily, but now information was compartmentalized and disseminated on a need to know basis only.

Since Mathew and Dillon were too young to join the army, according to Colonel Thomas, they passed the time watching the training or running errands for the rebels and their officers. Due to the rigorous training and substandard living conditions, many rebels had deserted. Some worried about their families; others just didn't like the new changes. They believed their "hit and run" method of warfare was best. They found many excuses to leave the compound and not return. If anything, this strengthened the regiment by eliminating the bad seeds. Complaints decreased and morale increased. The men were not only learning the fundamentals of urban warfare, but more importantly they were learning to function as a team. Each member was assigned a specific task, leading to an ultimate group goal. Just like pieces of a jigsaw puzzle, each individual piece had to fit exactly with each of the other pieces, so as to see the whole picture.

While filing some letters for Colonel Thomas one day, Mathew came across a discouraging one. Seeing Dillon in the next room, he waved him over. "Look at this," he said, keeping his voice low so others wouldn't notice them. Mathew kept watch as his friend read the letter.

> *Dear Colonel Thomas,*
> *As per your request for more weapons and ammunition; our answer currently is negative. We will not be able to fulfill your demands. Due to the loss of many of our weapons and the need for them in multiple locations throughout the United States, you will have to make do with what you procured before your departure. We are exceedingly destitute of automatic weapons as well as high-tech armament. You are ordered to make due and proceed in your missions as planned. We hope that you will be able to obtain necessary munitions and arms as you stage your attacks against the alien forces. We are cognizant of your predicament and offer our sincere apologies and best wishes for your success. The success and survival of our nation currently rests in the hands of a few capable officers and their units like yourselves. Good luck and God bless.*

The letter, short and to the point, was signed President Robert T. Morris, commander and chief, United States of America.

"Wow. That really sucks. Without weapons we don't stand a chance. How are we supposed to engage the enemy if we don't have any guns or bullets?" Dillon whispered.

"This is one of the main reasons it's so hard to find people to join the movement," Mathew said. "Who wanted to join, when they weren't even guaranteed a weapon? What were they supposed to fight with, rocks?"

Later that night, exhausted from his still-healing wound, his running around and his discovery of the president's letter, Mathew fell asleep as soon as he crawled into bed. It felt like minutes later when someone shook him awake.

"Mathew, Mathew, wake up!"

He was about to punch his way back to sleep when he recognized Dillon's voice. He opened his eyes. Dillon was leaning over him holding his rifle in his hands.

"What's going on? Are we under attack?" Mathew asked, reaching for his own weapon that was leaning against the wall. He had grown extremely fond of his weapon, to the point that it had become an extension of himself. He carried it almost everywhere he went, never knowing when he would need it. But because of the lack of ammunition, he couldn't practice any live firing. He had taken it apart and cleaned so many times, anyone would think it had just come off the assembly line. Always take care of your equipment, his father had counseled him and they will take care of you. The number one benefit of his weapon, he had to admit, was the jealous gleam in Dillon's eye. Compared to his relic, Mathew's weapon, although several years old, looked brand new. It was the high end BMW to Dillon's low end VW.

"No, just get your stuff and meet me outside," Dillon whispered.

By the time he collected his gear and went outside, Dillon was pacing excitedly. "Follow me and don't make a sound."

Together they started through camp, careful to avoid the sentries. It was a hot night, and they were sweating by the time they made their way to the perimeter. Dillon's excitement was palpable. Mathew was confused and slightly disoriented from being woken so abruptly. They continued their noiseless hike. Other than some crickets chirping and the occasional snore, they heard nothing as they made their way out of camp.

"Hey, hold up. Where are we going?" Mathew finally whispered.

"Shhh! Keep your voice down. We are going to see the Colonel," Dillon said, trying to sound cryptic and stern at the same time.

"The colonel, what for?!" He asked, peeved for the admonishment. He hadn't spoken any louder than necessary. He contemplated smacking Dillon in the head, just to voice his displeasure, but decided against it. He could tell how excited Dillon was even in the dark, so he forgave him his reproach, although he did file it away for future reference. If he let him get away with it, he'd mark it on his scorecard as a win. It was a game they had been playing for years, trying to one up each other or score some sort of smart-aleck jab whenever possible. Dillon was too smart to let him get away with it, especially on the easy ones. The guy had the memory of an elephant and could pull out something that happened years ago and make him swallow his "loser" pill twice. Mathew had experienced this several times and he was the first to admit that it "burned" worse the second time around.

CHAPTER 10

• • •

THEY LEFT THE COMPOUND, CLIMBING over a chain link fence. Mathew saw a jeep idling farther up the dirt road. As they silently approached it, he detected movement in the woods near the parked vehicle. Before he could say anything to Dillon, Major Myers stepped from behind a tree. Major Mike Myers had come to camp with the Colonel and was his second-in-command.

Lighting a cigarette, he said, "Evening, gentlemen, the Colonel is expecting you." As he took a drag of his cigarette he added, "These things will kill ya. Make sure you never develop the habit. I started when I was your age and haven't been able to kick the habit since. Follow me, please."

That's the least of my worries right now, Mathew thought. He was still confused over what was happening and Dillon was no help. Mathew detected a smirk on his friend's face. Not wanting to beg for more information, he kept his mouth shut and followed him. As they approached the jeep, the driver's side window went down and Colonel Thomas spoke. "Please join me, gentlemen."

Mathew's heart was beating a mile a minute as they climbed into the backseat. As he reached over to close the door, he saw a map in the Colonel's lap and noticed another man sitting on the passenger side next to him.

The man was saying, "--the aliens are heavily entrenched here and here. Boston in general is under siege. They have superior forces and hold strategic positions," pointing to spots on the map. "The mother ship is stationed at the airport, with General Moutari on board. Alien patrols are present in all districts, especially the North End and South Boston where the majority of the population is located. Boston proper has been mostly destroyed, few buildings are even standing, and most roads and avenues are either pockmarked by craters and holes or blocked by rubble and debris making it difficult to navigate any vehicles through."

The boys were taken by surprise, when the Colonel suddenly turned around and addressed them. "This is Jeffrey, one of our best scouts. As you heard things don't look good in Boston." The Colonel stared soberly at their sweaty faces. "How old are you boys?"

"Fourteen going on fifteen, sir!" they both said at the same time.

The Colonel turned to Jeffrey and said, "I don't like it, but desperate times call for desperate measures." Turning back to them, he said, "I heard you two are good, capable boys, who held their own during a battle with the alien force. One of you was wounded as I was told. You've not only stayed out of mischief, but you've made yourselves useful around camp. Several of my own men hold you in high regard. That is why I called you here tonight. I have an important mission that needs your particular skills, but I can't force you into it, especially if you're scared. In normal times I would never ask you to do anything like this, but the situation leaves me no choice."

"We're not scared!" they both answered.

"We'll do anything to help." Dillon said.

"I know, Dillon, if you're anything like your brother, I'm sure you will."

"You know my brother, sir?" Dillon asked proudly.

"Not personally I'm afraid, but I've read his reports and he seems highly capable and extremely motivated. His commanding officers praise him, and some of his missions were nothing short of amazing. Brian's someone I'd love to have in this regiment if I could."

"Thank you, sir," Dillon answered. "He'll be glad to hear it." Wait until he told Brian what the Colonel said, he'd be so happy he'd probably soil himself. Maybe that'd be the best time to get him to give him a better weapon than the piece of crap he currently had, he pondered. Even Mathew, the newbie, had a sweet AK-47, while he tinkered around with this World War II antiquity, he thought covertly eyeing his friend's weapon.

"Well, let me tell you the particulars of your mission, and then you can decide," Colonel Thomas continued. "I can't order you to do this, but I will say that no one would suspect you boys of working with the rebel forces, especially considering your age. I'm sure you've heard all the rumors concerning the current situation. All I can tell you is that bands of rebel forces have been harassing the aliens all over the country. They are in contact with our leaders in Washington and under direct secret orders from the president to harass and engage the alien forces whenever possible. The one big problem we are having is that our weapons are limited and in some regions of the country, almost nonexistent. General Moutari, the supreme leader of the Magar, has done a thorough job of confiscating or destroying our weapons and military arsenals. Even though we have accessed hidden weapon storage facilities throughout the country, we are still in desperate need of more, if we expect to defeat this alien threat." After taking a big breath, he continued. "It's for this reason I've asked you here tonight. If you decide to accept the mission, it might make a big difference in the survival of our rebel forces. If you decide to accept and carry out my orders, you will leave here and make your way back to Boston. One of our people will meet you on the road back and drive you as close to your destination as possible. If you happen to be stopped by alien patrols, you will pretend to be brothers." He solemnly looked in their direction, before continuing. "You were picked up by your uncle when your parents were killed during an air raid and are going to live with him and his family in Boston. Once there you need to find a certain man who calls himself Mr. Ryan. He was a police officer before the aliens took over. He is pretending to be an alien supporter and informer, but in reality he is a true patriot and very brave man, passing information to our side whenever he can. He somehow got word to our country's leaders that he has vital information that will help the rebel forces. It might be nothing. Or it might be the key to winning this war. Either way, we have to find out what it is."

"It might also be a trap. He could have been exposed or even turned," piped the scout.

"Yes, but we have to take the risk. We have no choice. So please, boys, think carefully before you answer," he said looking the two in the eye.

"So you want us to go meet this man and get the information he has?" Mathew asked.

"Yes, that's right. Then make your way back here as soon as possible. If you accept this mission, you will be on your own. All I can tell you is Mr. Ryan is known to frequent Faneuil Hall and the North End--areas I'm sure you're both familiar with. He takes long walks, like he used to do when he was on patrol. He is a tall, dark-haired, heavy set man. He walks with a slight limp, compliments of a bank robber, who tried to shoot his way out of a robbery. He has recently taken to using a cane with a solid silver handle in the shape of an eagle. That will be your key to recognizing him. That and a small scar below his eye in the shape of a teardrop."

At the mention of the word "scar," both boys averted their eyes, so as not to stare at the Colonel's own battle wound.

"So take a few minutes to discuss it amongst yourselves. You can take a walk or we can get out and stretch our legs if you need to be alone."

The boys nodded at each other, passing a silent message between them. After nodding to each other, they turned their attention back to the Colonel.

Dillon said, "We will accept your mission and follow your orders to the best of our abilities." "To be honest, we were trying to figure out a way to go back to Boston, sir. Our families must be worried sick, and we didn't think we were doing any good just hanging around."

"Well boys, all I can say is that I speak for the whole rebel force as I express my gratitude. You are doing a great service for your country. Good luck. You are going to need it. But no matter what happens, I want you to know how proud of you I am. If all the rebels had your courage and drive, we would have won this war a long time ago."

Once they received the remaining details, they returned to camp and promptly fell asleep. The next morning, after a quick breakfast and without saying a word to anyone, they set off toward Boston, having been shown their current location on the Colonel's map so they could return once they had obtained the information. They were surprised to find out that they were currently in New Hampshire, near the coast. The Colonel was unsure exactly where their driver would meet them, but they were to stay as close to the major expressways as possible.

Major Myers had replaced their weapons with smaller handguns, promising to safeguard and return them once the boys completed their mission. He also gave them each an extra clip. "These are easier to carry and also hide. Make sure the aliens don't find them on you or you'll be executed on the spot. Ever since the Battle of Charlestown, they aren't taking any chances." He also handed them a canteen and two Coke bottles full of water, as well as a handful of energy bars. Finally, he added a map, similar to the one they had studied the night before. "Notice that the map has no markings on it what so ever. Keep it that way, just in case you are captured or killed, there won't be anything to give our location away. You also won't be forced to answer questions on what the marks are. You can always say you have it to use as kindling for your fires. In the meantime you can use it as a reference, if you need to."

"You'd best be off as soon as you finish breakfast," said the Colonel as he walked up with the scout in tow. "It's best if you go while it's still dark out. Less eyes watching and all. Again good luck and god speed."

All three men shook the boys' hands before they set off for camp. And then in an unexpected gesture all three men saluted the boys.

It was getting high to noon, when the boys stepped off the road to take their second break of the morning. Squatting behind some shrubs, they rested. They had barely spoken to each other in hours, concentrating on covering as much ground as possible. As they shared the energy bars and water, Mathew asked, "When do you think our driver will meet up with us? I'm tired of walking."

"Me too. But your guess is as good as mine. At this pace, it'll take us at least a week to get home."

"We haven't seen a soul since we left the camp. Where is everyone?" Mathew wondered out loud.

"Don't forget, Mathew, a lot of people were killed during the initial invasion. Also, starvation and lack of proper medical care claimed hundreds of thousands more. You remember how hard it was to find food and medical supplies those first few months. It's only been recently that the aliens have released their miserly hold on the goods we need to survive. My brother says they did it because we were getting too weak to bury our own dead and they were too lazy to do it themselves. And, don't forget that they control and ration gasoline for our cars. Well, the cars that still work anyways. That electromagnetic pulse wave they released fried most of the electronics, not only in the telecommunication and social media networks but also in most new car models. You know they're based on electronics and memory chips and motherboards. I mean, hell, our microwave doesn't even work, and the only reason our stove still works is cause it runs on natural gas. My mom has to use a lighter or match to start it!"

"Yeah, I know. I was just saying," Mathew said guiltily, knowing he had upset his friend. "Sorry."

"Don't be sorry, dude; I'm just tired and a little scared, that's all. Plus the sun is getting to me. I swear I hear music."

Suddenly, Mathew also could hear music. Without warning they saw a car approaching, blaring *"Born to be Bad"* from its speakers. Cautiously, looking out from behind some bushes, they saw an old 1970s Trans-Am. It was jet black with t-tops and had the original emblem on the hood. The guy driving was the spitting image of Burt Reynolds in the ancient *Smokey and the Bandit* movies, straight down to his mustache and cowboy hat.

That was the only good thing about the electronics bar-b-cue that had occurred, Mathew thought, taking in the cars sleek lines and wide tires. You now got to see some real classics driving around. 2015 Porsche, my butt. Nothing like a 1968 Ford Mustang. One of his favorite cars of all time. Big fans of muscle car magazines and frequent visitors of all car exhibitions and museums, they each had their favorite make and model. Mathew had argued the Trans Am's merits with Dillon on many occasions, who was partial to the early Stingray Corvettes. They had even gone a week without talking after an especially intense debate. Finally making up, they had agreed to disagree, but this prime example of American ingenuity and engineering was sure to earn him some solid debate points in the future.

"I bet that's him. Let's go," Dillon said, admiring the car as it raced toward them, throwing clouds of dust into the air. Even though he would never admit it to Mathew, he was highly impressed and awed at the sheer power and presence of their intended chariot. To be honest he couldn't wait to get in and get on their way.

As they left the bushes and approached the road, the driver pulled over. Fishtailing as he slammed on the brakes, bringing several hundred horses to a complete stop, he stared at them through mirrored sunglasses. The car continued to growl, as its exhaust discharged levels of emissions not seen since the 1970s.

Lowering his window, he stated the obvious. "There's two of you. They said one. No matter. Jump in, we're behind schedule."

Dillon jumped in the back, as Mathew positioned himself in the front seat, fastening his seat belt and marveling at the immaculate interior. The Trans Am was two-door coupe that came standard with a 250 CID six-cylinder engine that produced 155 horsepower. You could upgrade to the Formula 400 version that came with a 400 CID V8 engine that produced 355 horsepower. The four-barrel engine could be modified to increase horsepower output. This car was the latter, and he could tell that the engine had been tweaked to provide even more power. This was a beast of an automobile. Along with its high performance engine, the car had power steering, power brakes, and Rally II wheels. The interior consisted of black on red bucket seats and was retrofitted with racing seat belt harnesses and stainless steel pedals. The standard steering wheel was replaced with a high-performance version, and he saw a gauge for a nitrous boost. This car could fly. In his opinion this was one of the best muscle cars the United States had ever produced and whoever had modified it really knew his stuff. And to think, you could buy it for only $4,300 back in the old days.

A moment later they were fishtailing back onto the road, gravel and dirt flying all over the place. Soon they found the highway and their driver really put the pedal to the metal. The boys were in heaven. They had huge smiles plastered on their faces as they were pinned to their seats. Momentarily forgetting their mission, they enjoyed the experience of doing 120 miles per hour in a 70's muscle car. Normally a two-hour drive, it took six with all the detours they had to take to avoid the destroyed asphalt and collapsed bridges.

They were approaching the outskirts of the city when their driver finally spoke. "Can't go too far from here, too many patrols. Don't need any hassles. I'll drop you off on Storrow Drive, and you can hoof it from there."

At last they came in view of Boston and continued south. Soon their driver pulled over and let them out. "Good luck," he said before pulling a U-turn and peeling off in the direction they had just come from.

He was out of sight before Mathew realized that they didn't even know his name. Turning toward the city, they started off on foot once again.

"Guy was a real chatter box, huh?" he joked. "But I have to say, that was one sweet ride." Suddenly serious Mathew asked, "So how are we going to do this?"

"I've been thinking of that since the colonel told us the mission. I think I should stay in the background while you approach Mr. Ryan and do all the talking. I'll keep under cover and look out for any danger or a double cross. Once we get what we need, we stop by our homes to say we're okay and then we figure out how to get back to New Hampshire as soon as possible."

"I guess that's what we'll do then," Mathew responded not having a better plan of his own.

"Just remember," Dillon added, "act as if I'm not around. Don't try to find me. Don't look for me. I promise, I'll be nearby watching your back. If anything funny goes down, I'll come in guns blazing."

"Easy there, Rambo. Whatever you do, just make sure you don't shoot me. One bullet wound is enough. Plus if any funny business goes down, I'm running away so fast all you're going to see is my dust. I swear to God, you put Usain Bolt next to me and I'll leave him so far behind, you'd think he was a one-legged fat man with a chronic gout condition."

Laughing, Dillon said, "Let's get going, Speedy Gonzales. We're running out of light."

CHAPTER 11

• • •

FOLLOWING STORROW DRIVE, THEY ENTERED the North
End by the old Fleet Center. "This is where we split up.
Good luck," Dillon said. Bumping fists, he crossed the
street and disappeared down an alley. Taking a deep
breath, Mathew made his way to Atlantic Avenue, where
he started looking around for their contact. As he crossed
over toward Hanover Street, he encountered an alien
patrol. Trying to act normal, he continued walking till he
was ordered to stop.

"Halt!" an alien in full combat gear yelled, barring his
way with his laser rifle.

Mathew stopped. Heart pounding, he was conscious
of the weapon poking his chest through his shirt. He stood
quietly waiting for the alien patrol leader to address him.

"What are you doing, boy? Are you looking for trouble?
You're not one of those terrorists, are you?" he demanded.

"No sir. My mom's sick and I'm looking for medicine," he replied thinking quickly. He should have had
a story ready, he chided himself. "I'm on the way to the

pharmacy, sir. If you don't mind, sir, I need to get there before they close."

The alien laughed at his awkwardness. "They should all be this respectful. It's time these humans bowed to their new masters," he growled to his fellow unit members, who guffawed in return. "Get along, boy, before I change my mind and use you for target practice."

Mathew thanked him and set off at a run. But before he could get too far, the alien's voice brought him to a halt.

"STOP! What's your name boy? And where do you live, for that matter," the alien asked in that guttural manner that passed for alien loquacity. He would have to report the encounter and didn't want to be reprimanded for not having questioned the subject completely.

"Uhh--my name's Mathew and I live on Prince Street," he answered, remembering where he was. Prince Street still housed many people, one of the few streets that had not been destroyed in the attacks. Other than some broken windows and cracks in the brick veneers the street stood, as if impervious to its ruined surroundings.

"Make sure we don't find you out after dark, boy, or else we won't be so nice. Do you understand me?"

"Yes, sir," Mathew replied, quickly taking off before they could ask him any more questions.

The whole time he was wondering where Dillon was. He must have slipped by the patrol while Mathew held the alien's attention. All the times they played ninja warriors were paying off. He was always touting his stealth skills and now he was putting his money where his mouth was.

They had been taking karate and jujitsu since they were young and Dillon always said their sensei, Master Hunn, was a secret ninja. Maybe he was right and all those extra hours Dillon had spent training with the sensei were paying off.

Mathew wanted to look around for him but refrained and stuck to the plan. It was getting dark out and most people were returning to their homes and shelters. He saw more and more alien patrols, but was lucky enough to avoid most of them. When he was stopped and questioned, he gave them the same story. He continued to search for the man with the limp. Near the waterfront, he was surprised to see more people. These were sailors and merchant marines and wharf rats. They were loading and unloading goods and supplies on mostly old vessels and fishing boats under the supervision of the alien authorities, who were on the lookout for weapons and contraband.

Guess that electronic pulse also took out seafaring vessels as well as land and air transportation, Mathew thought, to himself. He wondered if he was going to find his contact today or if they would have to do this again tomorrow. His eyes searched all over. He explored dark alleys and peered into windows. He searched the shadows of recessed doorways and isolated trees and shrubs. Once, he caught a glimpse of Dillon and felt safer knowing that his friend was still there. The men and women about were rough and crude and did more arguing amongst themselves than actual work.

He had wandered into a sort of fish market. The pungent smell masked the odor of hundreds of unwashed bodies. Who would have ever thought soap and toilet paper would become such hot commodities? Even here, he noticed armed patrols eyeing the crowds and individuals with suspicion, many times searching nets and buckets of fish for any hidden items. If anyone protested their search, they were roughly beaten to the ground and left to wither in pain, their catch seized and thrown back into the ocean as further punishment. Laughing and joking, the aliens would then continue their patrol as if nothing had happened. More times than not, they left behind not battered and bruised victims but bloody lifeless corpses.

Mathew eventually came to a long shack on one of the piers that had the word "BAR" painted on the front wall. It was made of rough unpainted wood boards and rusted metal sheets. Windowless on all but one side, the bar had a pipe on the sloped metal roof that acted as a chimney stack. The roof was painted white and gray with pigeon and seagull droppings. The door was no more than three wide vertical wood boards held together by two horizontal slabs of the same metal sheets that made up the roof and majority of the building. A braided rope acted as a doorknob and locking mechanism. Should he go in and check? He was scared to go into a place like that but he didn't think he had a choice. Watching two men exit, he reached the door before it closed. He stepped inside before he could talk himself out of it. Taking a step to his right to get out of the way, he surveyed the room.

It was dingy and long, noisy and full of smoke. It smelled of fish, vomit and noxious body odor. The air hung thick and fetid like rank cheese. Mathew held his breath as he looked around. Fortunately, nobody seemed to notice him. If they did, they didn't care. He didn't see his intended subject and was about to leave when someone in the corner caught his attention. He tried to see through the smoke. Halting and reversing his retreat he edged deeper into the room. Looking around the mass of bodies, he attempted to get a better view of his wished-for contact. Catching a glimpse of a heavyset man holding a cane, he headed in that direction. Cutting his way through the crowd and smoke he made his way to the corner where he had glimpsed the man with the cane. As he was going around a mountain of a man, a behemoth to be exact, arms reached out and lifted him right off the ground.

"Well, well, looky looky now. What do we have here? Wanting to go to sea, are ya? I got a berth for you, but you're going to have to work hard for your keep. My dear old Skipper Maurice doesn't take kindly to slackers. He's been known to revert to the old nine-tails for proper motivation," chortled the biggest man Mathew had ever seen.

Almost fainting from the inebriated stench that escaped the giant's lips, Mathew couldn't help thinking that a roll of mints couldn't help this guy. He was considering about making some sort of comment, but the sheer size of the guy had anchored his tongue in place. The guy was the NBA's Kareem Abdul Jabar, the WWE's The Rock, and the WWF's Andre the Giant rolled into one. This guy was an NBA dunking, wrestling body-slamming circus freak.

"Leave the boy alone, Tiny! You're scaring him!" yelled someone from a nearby table.

Tiny? Tiny? Was the guy blind? Mathew wondered. This guy was huge. He could have been the poster child for why PEDs do a body good. His arm was bigger than his whole body. He was gi-normous! He was a transformer on steroids for god's sake. Mathew looked wildly about him. The guy's vice-like grip squeezed him so tight his head was going to pop off. Frustrated and unable to move, Mathew glanced around helplessly. Then all of a sudden, the big oaf put him down and returned to his drink without saying another word.

Quickly moving away from the giant, Mathew searched for the man that had yelled at "Tiny" and saved his life. The least he could do was thank him. As he moved toward the table the voice had come from, he realized that it was the man with the cane who had yelled out in his defense. Seeing the cane with its eagle handle against the table, he continued to make his way in that direction. The tear-shaped scar below his eye confirmed the man's identity.

"Thanks. That guy almost snapped me in half," Mathew offered trying to catch his breath and settle his nerves. "That guys a menace to society. If Godzilla had a brother that guy would be covered in scales and sporting a tail. He can't even stand straight up for fear of blocking out the sun," Mathew continued trying to vent himself free of the fear he had just experienced.

"Don't mention it. Tiny's harmless. He just doesn't know his own strength," the man replied, amused. "He didn't mean anything by it and probably won't remember any of it tomorrow. He lost some family and friends at the *Battle of Charlestown* and is trying to drown his sorrows. Another day or two and he'll snap out of it. You can't find answers at the bottom of a bottle. God knows I've tried," he said with a pensive look on his face.

"If you say so. But I'd rather not go through that again, if it's all right with you," Mathew added as he regained some decorum.

The man laughed, his face completely transformed from its previous look, as he asked, "What are you doing here boy? You should be home. This is no place for children."

"Looking for you, sir, if your name's Mr. Ryan," Mathew replied, hurt by the unintended slight.

Arching his eyebrows he asked, "Is that so?"

"Yes, sir. Can we go outside and talk? It's very noisy in here and what I have to say is private."

Without another word, but with an amused look in his eye, the man got up, grabbed his cane, and went outside. Mathew, hot on his heels, hoped he had the right man. What were the chances there'd be two people with an eagle cane and tear drop scar? Once outside they moved farther along the pier, until they found a quiet spot beneath a broken lamppost.

"Don't tell me he sent you?"

"If you mean Colonel Thomas, then the answer is yes. I'm supposed to return to him with your message," Mathew half whispered. He glanced around to make sure they were alone and it wasn't some sort of trap.

"What's your name?"

"Mathew."

The heavyset man gazed across the water for a moment before saying, "Then you and I should have a chat. Now, boy, what do you know about the rebel forces? I was expecting a full-grown man, not some wet-behind-the-ears little boy."

Mathew tried to keep his cool as he said, "I was at the Battle of Charlestown, sir. There's some dead aliens I sent to their maker. I might be young but I haven't been wet behind the ears for some time now. It would behoove you to watch yours manners, so I don't grab your cane and beat you over the head with it." Mathew ended, unable to help himself. He was hungry, tired, and on edge. Everything he had gone through--the fighting, the running, the getting shot, his mission to get here all added up, the tension was too much to hold in, especially after that unjustified provocation. So, in his opinion, this former police detective with the limp and ungrateful attitude became the legitimate recipient of his bad-mannered but warranted rant.

Authentic surprise and shame came over Ryan's face, and he said, "Sorry kid. I'm just venting. I had no right to say what I said. But I've been undercover so long my nerves are shot. If Colonel Thomas trusted you with this mission, then I should have kept my opinions to myself. I'm sorry again."

"I'm sorry also for threatening to beat you over the head with your cane, but I've been through a lot lately and lost my cool. I hope you know I would never do that to you."

"What would you have done, if I had continued to berate you," asked the former police detective with an amused look on his face.

"Oh that's easy. I would have shot you in your good leg," Mathew replied with a big smile plastered on his face. The current tension defused, he continued, "Sir, with all due respect, I need to get back as soon as possible. To be perfectly honest, I've been stopped too many times by aliens today for my luck to hold out. So if you can please explain everything you need, I promise to relay the information to Colonel Thomas to the best of my abilities."

"Did you come alone, Mathew?"

"No sir, my friend Dillon is out there somewhere acting as backup, as well as an early warning system."

"Well, I'll be damned," he said. "Okay, then pay attention. I came across some vital information, essential to the rebel forces. The Magars are about to move an enormous supply of confiscated weapons and munitions. There's enough to supply the rebel forces all over the country for months."

Mathew stared excitedly at his companion. He wanted to ask a million questions, but bit his tongue. He would let Mr. Ryan tell his story.

"Like I said, I've been undercover a long time, acting as an informer and traitor. I've gotten so close to General Moutari himself, that I'm even allowed access to his ship. One day, while I was snooping around I heard the general and his lieutenants discussing the need to move the confiscated weapons. Some advocated destroying them but the general said they might come in handy during future rioting and unrest, or even on other world invasions. He said that some worlds were capable of defending against their plasma and laser armament, but would be hard-pressed to counter these primitive weapons with their projectile abilities. Anyway, other than learning that we are not alone in the universe and that the Magars are on a mission to conquer all the worlds in the solar system, I was able to get more details. There are enough weapons to distribute to rebel forces all over the country. Supply all our forces for months. If their convoy can be intercepted and captured, the Colonel's problems would be solved. Now pay attention while I give you the details of the route the aliens will take and all other relevant information. But be careful this information only goes to the Colonel. There are a lot of spies around. People will do anything to garner favors and supplies from the Magars."

Mathew listened closely as Mr. Ryan repeated the specifics over and over. Mathew repeated the information back, verbatim. During his fifth regurgitation, of all pertinent facts, routes, coordinates, enemy strengths and weaknesses, as well as all alien weaponry details, they heard a large commotion at the top of the pier. There was shouting, yelling, and a trampling of boots. As the noise increased, Mathew saw people running away in different directions.

A door slammed and a gunshot echoed. Mathew gaped. In an instant the pier lit up like a Christmas tree. Alien ships were flying overhead and alien patrol boats bobbed on the water. Their lights lit up the area as if it were daytime. All at once Dillon came charging down the pier, yelling to be heard over the alien's favorite broadcast blaring over and over: "Disobedience will be punished!"

"Come on, we have to move," Dillon yelled. "Bad guys comin! Go! Go! Go!"

As Dillon reached them, Mathew and Mr. Ryan stared in stunned silence watching the chaos unfold. No time for questions. Aliens were racing in their direction. Dillon grabbed his arm pulling him along. "Got to go! Got to go," he kept yelling.

"Halt! Halt!" yelled the alien patrol charging in their direction. Brandishing their weapons, they started to fire indiscriminately, not caring who or what they hit.

"Disobedience will be punished!" blared the ships overhead.

Ricocheting bullets and pieces of pier soaring all around them, the three covered their faces with their arms to avoid being hit. The place was in an uproar. Aliens firing weapons, people running to escape, ships blaring, people screaming, it was total chaos. Mathew saw that Mr. Ryan had disappeared. Looking toward Dillon, he saw his friend had his gun in his hand. Aiming while running, he shot out several lamps. As the lights blew out, sparks rained down, but they were eventually shrouded in shadows. Zigzagging, finding cover behind anything they could, they made their way down the length of the pier.

The aliens continued on. "Halt, Halt!" they roared while they discharged their weapons in their direction. Suddenly, an alien came at them at a run. Startled by this unexpected maneuver, the boys froze. He was one out of a group of three that had pursued them down the pier. The one benefit was that he blocked his fellow soldier's ability to shoot without the fear of hitting him also. Swinging his weapon at Dillon's head, he momentarily lost his balance, skidding to a halt. Dillon ducked, barely avoiding the alien rifle and saving himself a crushed skull. Snapping out of his haze, Mathew looked around for some sort of weapon. He knew he couldn't shoot without hitting Dillon, so he did the next best thing. He hefted a good-size rock or piece of concrete, took a few steps, and pelted the rock at the alien. He missed and nearly hit Dillon instead.

"Hey," yelled Dillon, "we're on the same team!" Lunging to get away from his assailant, he tripped on the uneven planks and fell, dropping his gun. Scrambling to recover, he shuffled backward, doing his best to avoid the alien swinging his weapon like a Louisville slugger. Where was this guy when the Red Sox needed a cleanup hitter, Dillon thought, as he avoided another swing that would have been declared a grand slam if it had made contact with his head.

Mathew threw another chunk of rock at the alien. He scored a hit as the alien was about to reach Dillon. The alien's visor fractured, momentarily blinding him. Dillon scrambled away on all fours and retrieved his weapon.

He threw himself backward as the two remaining aliens joined the fight. Mathew tripped and fell, avoiding a gloved roundhouse punch by the closer of the two invaders. The alien who threw the missed punch came on waving a laser weapon that was coming dangerously close to Mathew's personal space. Going around the still struggling alien with the broken visor, he fired his weapon, the beam narrowly missing Mathew's arm and hitting the ground next to him. Gravel stung as it hit him across the face and neck. That's going to leave a mark, he thought as he scrambled to get away.

Still Mathew felt the jolt down to his toes. The proximity of the alien and the near miss almost made him wet himself. He slammed his head against the ground trying to scramble away and felt blood edge into his collar. Coming out of nowhere, Dillon tackled the alien behind the knees, dropping him to the ground. Jumping up before the alien could regain his feet; he kicked him as hard as he could in the head felling him again.

As the alien with the fractured helmet was finally able to pull it off, he was greeted by an especially heavy rock to the head, thrown by Mathew who had regained his own feet. His alien knocked unconscious, Mathew found Dillon engaged with the third and final aggressor. He had confiscated the felled alien's laser gun and was currently shooting it at anything and everything that moved. Keeping the third alien pinned down behind a pile of concrete and rubble; they ran farther down the pier. Shooting out lights as they went along, they tried to put as much distance between themselves and the alien soldiers. The darkness gained them a few precious seconds, but time was running out. They were reaching the end of the pier and had to find a way off or they were toast.

"What do we do? - jump?" Mathew asked panting heavily, trying to staunch the flow of blood running down his neck with one hand, and wiping the blood from his eyes with the other. He couldn't tell what hurt more the blow to his head or the gravel to his face. He really needed to stop using himself as a human target, it was getting excruciatingly painful.

"Guess so," Dillon said as they raced on. "How's your head? It's really bleeding a lot. I bet it hurts."

"It feels like I went a few rounds with Mike Tyson and lost. I can tell you the pounding is worse than the pain."

Suddenly, they saw Mr. Ryan waving to them from the end of the dock. He seemed to be hanging in air, waiting for them. He was standing on a ladder that led down to the rocky shore. They weren't safe yet. They had to move quickly. Dillon in the lead, they followed the detective down the ladder. He was going so fast, he almost tumbled head first off the pier. Mathew almost missed the ladder rungs himself, but regained his balance and made it down safely, barely avoiding stepping on Dillon's fingers below him.

"This way," yelled Mr. Ryan. "We might have to fight it out. Do you have any weapons?"

"Yes!" They said together, showing him their guns. Mathew with his automatic nine millimeter and Dillon with his recently acquired alien laser and handgun.

Impressed, Mr. Ryan advised them to keep them handy because they might need them shortly. "This might get ugly, boys, so lock and load."

• • •

STOPPING TO CATCH THEIR BREATHS and to familiarize themselves with their surroundings, they stood still, the boys silent. Mr. Ryan wheezed and coughed trying to get his lungs to catch up to his need for more air.

"What happened?" asked Mathew looking at Dillon. "Why did all the Magars show up at once? Where did they all come from?"

"Beats me! One minute nothing, next thing I know it's raining aliens. They started flooding the pier like rats. They were coming out of the shadows, as if they were made of smoke," he said still catching his breath. "Then all of a sudden bullets were flying, people were screaming, and that darn announcement started blaring over and over. 'Disobedience will be punished! Disobedience will be punished!' I swear if I'd seen that ship, I'd have blasted it out of the air. I'm so sick of listening to that thing. Someone has to tell them that variety is the spice of life. They should mix it up a little bit, maybe add a little music or change the warning to, 'Bad People Will Get Spanked.'

For a second there, I thought of shooting myself, just so I wouldn't have to listen to it any longer."

"One of the patrols must have noticed something suspicious or it was a planned raid so as to continue to instill fear and doubt in the unruly and often troublesome sailors and dock workers. Maybe they got wind of illegal contraband. It probably doesn't even have to do with us. It was too dark for them to make out our faces, anyway. They just saw three people running down the pier and followed. I doubt, they were tracking you. In any case, they saw us."

"Here, use this," Mr. Ryan said, handing Mathew a handkerchief to help stop the bleeding. "Are you hurt bad?"

"No, I'm fine. Just a bump," Mathew said, wincing as he applied pressure to the wound.

"What are you guys, midget comedians? You should take your act on the road. I haven't heard so many one-liners since Eddie Murphy came to town."

Dillon said, "Don't worry about Mathew. His head is as hard as a rock. His noggin's taken so many lumps lately, it's a wonder he still knows his name." Dillon slapped Mathew on the back. "I think he does it for the attention. He's a real ladies' man, quiet but deadly. You should ask him about his current squeeze, Molly. She's a real babe," he continued while ducking Mathew's blow.

"I told you, she's not my girlfriend," Mathew said half-heartedly, too tired to argue.

"I can't tell if you guys are clueless or priceless," Mr. Ryan said shaking his head as if he couldn't believe that they were more interested in irking each other than comprehending the severity of their situation. Little did he know, how close they were and how this was their way of coping with dangerous and awkward situations.

As they stood there, back to back to back, they checked their weapons and mentally prepared themselves for more battle. Secretly, they all hoped there was some other way out of their predicament, but chances were they wouldn't make it off the beach alive. Each lost in his own thoughts, they waited for the inevitable.

Hidden in the shadows and pillars of the pier, Mathew remembered coming here with his parents to fish and clam. Never really caught much but it was fun to bait hooks and dig in the sand. One time his mother found a gold coin buried in the sand. Thinking there was more treasure, they had kept digging until nightfall, not finding anything else but having lots of fun nonetheless. They spent half the time wondering what they'd do with all the money they'd make selling the treasure. Now, Mathew wondered if they would ever experience those carefree times again. Or were they doomed to live under the rule of the Magars, their lives consisting of indentured servitude and uncertain survival?

"We have to move. Let's go-" Mr. Ryan said, finally having gotten enough oxygen to stave off death, at least for a little while longer.

"Whoa there, mister, not for nothing, but where are we going? And how do we know we can even trust you? How do we know you aren't leading us into some sort of trap?" asked Dillon.

"To answer your second and third questions first, you don't. To answer your first: I suggest we get below the pier and follow it back up to the road. We move quickly and quietly. If we get noticed, follow my lead and do exactly as I say." He turned to stare at both of them. "Gentlemen, you don't have a choice. You can trust me, or you can go off on your own. Either way I'm getting out of here."

Exchanging a quick glance, the boys knew they didn't have much of a choice. They needed to get as far away as possible from the mayhem and madness. "Okay, let's go," Dillon said suspicion still evident in his voice.

Mathew said, "Hold on for a second. Dillon, in case we get separated or something happens to me, you have to get back to the Colonel and tell him there's going to be a big weapons convoy." Mathew shared the details with Dillon, as Mr. Ryan silently urged them to hurry. Footsteps and voices could be heard above them, as the aliens located the ladder down to the beach.

Ducking low to avoid the searchlights currently illuminating the beach, they set off. Dodging rocks, debris, and broken dock support struts, they made their way closer and closer to the head of the pier. They could see spotlights shining through the wooden boards above them and heard hundreds of aliens traipsing like a herd of blind elephants, looking for a bag of peanuts. Fires burned above them as the occasional explosion rocked the pier. They weren't taking any chances; they were destroying everything. The "Bar" was a pile of ashes and the small stands and cabins dotting the pier and surrounding area were razed to the ground. Who knew how many human bodies littered the area? The sounds from the alien aircraft crisscrossing the vicinity were deafening. They walked, half crawled forward, trying to avoid the falling debris. It was literally raining concrete and wood. They had to stop and hide several times as alien aircraft shined their lights under the pier checking for survivors. The one good thing was that the aliens checking the beach had moved off in the opposite direction and were no longer a threat from behind.

"Disobedience will be punished," blared over and over. The sound repetitive and deafening. Masters at conquering and subjugating worlds, the Magars continued their psychological warfare. The constant barrage of loud and continuous threats was just as damaging to the human psyche as the physical violence was to the human body. By hampering the will to rebel, they continued to exert control by squashing the ideas of freedom and choice.

"Stay close now," whispered Mr. Ryan. As they came to the end, they crouched amongst the boulders below the entrance to the pier. Originally placed to act as a sea-wall, they now acted like a hiding hole for the three rebels. "Easy now. We wait for the right opportunity and then we make a run for that building," he said pointing to the end of the street, at an old brownstone with blown out windows. "Once there, we go around back and jump the fence. That will put us on another street. That's where we separate. You go right and I'll go left. Get out of town and back to the Colonel, ASAP!"

The boys nodded.

"Remember, if we get captured, let me do all the talking. The aliens know me. I will tell them that I've captured you and was bringing you to them. Look scared and keep your mouths shut!"

When the coast was clear they dodged out from under the pier onto the road and took off running toward the building. "Go, go, go," Mathew urged. They raced down the street, Mathew and Dillon in the lead. The heavy-set Mr. Ryan was huffing and puffing as if he had just run a marathon. His legs pumping for all he was worth, he looked as if he were running drills on a football field. Knees to chest, back straight, head up, eyes forward. He was holding his cane in one hand, a gun in the other, his arms flapping like wings on a drunk bird as he tried to gain as much speed as possible. If the situation were not so dire, Mathew would have probably fallen over laughing.

As they came up to the building, they stopped to wait for Mr. Ryan, but he waved them on. Turning on their heels they took off around the corner. In an alley, they climbed over a fence as if they were monkeys. They dropped down onto their haunches to catch their breaths and wait for Ryan. Five minutes later, Mr. Ryan dropped over the fence. The boys quickly turned away as Mr. Ryan emptied the contents of his stomach all over his shoes.

Trying hard not to laugh, they waited quietly, keeping their eyes on the road. They didn't see anything to arouse suspicion. It seemed all the action was on the other street by the docks.

"All right, follow the street and it will eventually take you out of the area. Just keep going north and get back to the Colonel," Mr. Ryan said spitting the last dregs of his dinner from between his teeth.

"We were going to visit our families after we made contact with you. We haven't seen them in a while and they're worried sick about us," Dillon said.

"Well, change of plans. Get the information to the rebel forces as soon as possible. They need to prepare if they're going to attempt to seize it."

"But we--"

"Listen, kids. This is war. Too many people are dying and this is an immense opportunity to score a major blow against these things that have tortured us for over a year." Seeing the boy's crushed expressions, he relented. "Okay, give me your addresses and I promise to go talk to your families myself. That's the best I can do."

After giving him their information they shook hands and took off in the direction he had pointed to. Knowing they wouldn't make it home was devastating, but deep down they knew their mission took priority. They took off at a run trying to cover as much distance as possible. Dodging holes and fallen buildings, they moved quickly through the growing darkness. They were almost out of the waterfront district when they ran into a Magar soldier. Invisible in the shadows, he had been leaning against a building. He stepped out and grabbed both by the collars of their shirts as they went by.

"Where are you going?" he growled, yanking both boys off their feet.

Frightened out of their wits, the boys just stood there mutely, sweating profusely, more out of fear than exertion. Shocked by the suddenness of the whole situation, they remained quiet. Unable to utter a word, they looked to each other for support.

"You're with the rebels. You will remain still while I contact my superiors," the alien said as he activated the communication device clipped to his chest. "Sector 6 reporting."

"Go Sector 6," a disembodied voice responded.

"I just caught two young humans running through my sector. Possible rebels. Request instructions."

"Interrogate and exterminate," the boys heard the eerie voice say. As the alien reached for his weapon, Mathew found his voice.

"Wai---t! Wait! We're not rebels. We're just kids!" Looking up into the alien's face, Mathew saw contempt and disgust mirrored in its eyes. He tried again. Thinking fast, he said, "Please, you don't understand. We are just going home. We were out and lost track of time. Our families must be worried sick. We just want to go home," he whined, hoping to elicit some sort of sympathetic response.

"You lie," yelled the alien, pointing his weapon at the boys. "What are you really up to? SPEAK! What is your mission! ANSWER ME!"

"We--we don't have a mission," Dillon replied, with a tremble. "My friend and I were watching the boats in the harbor. We were about to head home when the aliens--I mean the Magars attacked the pier. We were cut off and had to wait to head home. That's why we were running. Our parents will kill us for being late. Please, please just let us go."

"We live just up ahead. Please," Mathew implored, his fear returning as he realized that their pleas had fallen on deaf ears.

"Liars! Time to die." The alien said in a gravelly voice, filled with suspicion and apathy.

Just as he was about to squeeze the trigger of his weapon, a large explosion sounded. Startled, the alien turned toward the noise. The boys broke free from his grip. They both reached for the alien at the same time, pushing him as hard as they could. The alien fell over, his gun flying out of his hand and clattering along the street.

"Run!" yelled Mathew.

They fled down the street. They were nearing the next corner when laser beams started flying. The alien soldier was firing at them with a vengeance. Fragments of concrete from an adjacent building pelted the boys as they rounded the corner. The wild screams of the Magar echoing in their ears, they ran as fast as their legs would carry them. On and on they ran losing themselves in the alleys and side streets. On the edge of exhaustion, they finally stopped to rest.

"What do we do now? That alien has probably sounded the alarm and called in reinforcements. There's no way we are getting out of the city tonight," Dillon gasped.

"I know, I know. We have to find a place to lay low till things calm down," Mathew replied, bent over, hands on his knees trying to catching his breath. Finally, standing he looked around. A streetlight down the street illuminated the surrounding area. Dillon was leaning against a wall, eyes closed. Sweat covered his face and his shirt was soaked through. Taking a look around, Mathew was surprised to find himself in familiar surroundings. "Hey, Dillon, look."

Dillon opened his eyes. "What?"

"Not at me, stupid!" Mathew pointed in front of him.

Too tired to come back with a witty retort, Dillon looked around and gasped. "Holy cow, Mathew. We're in your neighborhood. We can crash at your house till tomorrow. You get to see your mom and your girlfriend Molly and I get to eat some of your mom's delicious cooking," he said, all of a sudden forgetting his exhaustion and finding his comedic flair.

"Shut up! You know she's not my girlfriend. We're just friends," Mathew said, although unconvincingly. "Let's go. Let's get off the street. I already see more patrols out."

"Lead the way, kimosabi. I'm right behind you," Dillon said laughing, his exhaustion temporarily forgotten.

Through the dark, deserted streets they crept. It was late. It had to be after midnight. Reaching Mathew's street they stopped to investigate the area. The last thing they needed was to get caught this close to the finish line or, god forbid lead the alien patrols to Mathew's home. They checked up and down the street, into all the doorways, and listened for footsteps. When they were finally sure there wasn't anyone around, they made a run for the building's front doors.

As they cleared the front entrance, Mathew took the lead, heading for the stairway, since the elevators were not working. His elation propelled him, faster and faster. It felt as if he hadn't been home in years. All he wanted to do was hug his mom and drop into his bed and sleep for a week.

"Hey, hold up. My legs are water, dude." Dillon panted behind him.

In his excitement to be home Mathew had left Dillon two flights back. "Sorry, dude. Didn't realize you were so out of shape," he said turning around before Dillon could see his smirk. "I'll slow down for you. I know how scared of the dark you are," he said chalking up another point.

"Bite me--," Dillon blurted as he put on a burst of speed.

Catching up to Mathew, he was surprised to find him just standing there. The door to his floor was in front of him, yet he just stood there. "What's wrong?" he asked suddenly weary of a trap. The empty hallway was illuminated by the moon shining through the window.

"What do we tell my mom? She's going to kill me," Mathew whispered.

Holding the door open with one hand and pushing him through with the other, Dillon laughed. "I bet all she does is hug you and cry. Now man up, alien hunter, and knock on the door. I'm hungry."

Softly knocking on the door, trying not to wake the neighbors, Mathew stood back waiting impatiently for his mother to open it. "Mom, it's Mathew," he whispered just loud enough for her to hear if she were standing behind the door.

The next thing he knew, his mom was hugging him so hard he swore he felt a rib snap. "Mom, I missed you so much," he said, tears clouding his eyes, returning her hug twice as tightly.

"I missed you, too, you crazy boy. Oh goodness, hello Dillon," Mom said, wiping away tears. Hugging Dillon just as hard, she urged them out into the apartment. "Tell me everything! Are you hurt? Are you thirsty? Hungry? Do you want to rest?"

"Easy Mom, take a breather and we'll tell you everything."

"Speak for yourself, bubba. I'm starving!" Dillon said heading for the kitchen. "You mind if I make myself at home, Mrs. H?" he said opening cupboard doors and slamming draws.

Laughing, Mom hurried to take control of his search before he destroyed her kitchen. "Just sit down and rest while I make some sandwiches. First you'll eat, and then you can tell me what happened. After that I'm going to kill both of you!"

As Mathew was about to follow, a knock came at the door. Mathew opened the door without thinking. Suddenly a waiflike figure slammed into him. He was about to defend himself when he realized that the thing hanging from his neck was Molly. She was wearing a long white nightgown and her hair was a mess. Her blue eyes filled with tears.

"Oh, Mathew. You're back. I thought I heard your voice. I thought I was dreaming at first, but then I heard your mom's voice and knew I had to find out what was going on. Why didn't you call? We were worried sick!" she said, still clinging to his neck.

Why didn't I call, seriously? Sometimes girls just didn't make any sense. "Uuhh, cause the phones don't work," he said, stating the obvious.

"I know, I know. I'm just happy you're back," she said finally letting go of his neck.

"Hey, Molly. Waz'up?" Dillon asked, a sandwich in his hand and a smirk on his face. "Do I get a hug like Mathew's?"

Molly rushed over and gave him a hug. Although it wasn't as long as Mathews, she followed up with a kiss on the cheek. Mathew felt his cheeks flush, as he experienced his first ever feelings of jealously. He felt like punching Dillon's smug face, but before he could act on his urges, his mother called them all into the kitchen where she had put together a late night feast.

As Mathew followed everyone into the kitchen, he thought back to the first time he had met Molly. It was the day after they had moved in. He was eager to start the new day, at his new school, excited about seeing Dillon again. Once breakfast was done, he had told his mother he would be downstairs waiting for her. Even though he knew he wouldn't score any "cool points" walking to school with his mother, he didn't have a choice. She had to sign all the necessary paperwork. Grabbing his school bag, he raced out the door hoping to have a few minutes alone to scope out the morning activity in his neighborhood. He raced down the four flights of stairs, too excited to wait for the elevator. Throwing open the stairwell door, he ran full tilt into the foyer and smack into Molly who, at that moment, happened to be walking out of the building herself. His momentum knocked both of them to the ground, book bags flying into the air, rear ends smacking the marble floor.

"Ouch!"

"I'm so sorry...," Mathew stammered.

Looking up into the bluest eyes, he remained tongue-tied. Before him was the prettiest girl he had ever seen. She had blond hair down to her shoulders, a freckle-sprayed button nose and the cutest dimples. Dressed in blue jeans, Ugg boots and a white tee, she could have been a model for Abercrombie Kids stores.

"Is there a fire?" she asked a wry grin on her face.

"Uh, no, uh, I mean, uh, I'm sorry. I didn't mean to run into to you. Sorry."

Laughing she said, "Don't worry about it. Are you new here? I'm Molly."

"I'm Mathew," he said, getting up, trying to salvage his reputation. "Let me get your bag," he added, while picking up her backpack and handing it to her.

"I live on the fourth floor. What about you?"

"I live on four, too," he replied. "We just moved in yesterday."

"Are you going to school? Do you want to walk together?" she asked shyly.

"Uh, uh, I have to go to school with my mom. It's my first day and she has to sign me up," he said hoping his face wasn't too red. "But you can walk with us, if you want."

"Sounds like fun. You sure your mom won't mind?"

"No, she's cool like that," he answered, praying his mother wouldn't embarrass him further.

He was frantically trying to think of something clever to say when the elevator doors opened and his mother walked off. Seeing Mathew and Molly standing there, she said hello.

"Hello, I'm Molly. I live on your floor."

"I'm Mrs. Holloway, Mathew's mom. Nice to meet you."

"You too."

"We should get going, if we don't want to be late," Mom said as she held open the door.

Mathew barely got a word in during that walk to school, his mother and Molly doing all the talking. But he and Molly became close friends over the years, walking to school together every day. They spent time together after school doing homework or just hanging out. To this day, Mathew credited his "cool factor" to the fact that he hung around with the prettiest girl in school.

Even Dillon was impressed that first day, when he walked onto the school grounds with Molly at his side. "Dude, how'd you do it? You haven't been here twenty-four hours and you're already hanging out with the coolest girl at school. That's what I call a player!" Dillon said, bumping fists. "Let me introduce you to the guys."

Now sitting at the table, Mathew realized how exhausted he was. He couldn't wait to eat and go to bed. After filling up on the first homemade meal they had in weeks, the boys filled Mom and Molly in on their adventures. They took turns telling their story and it was almost light out by the time they finished. By then they could hardly keep their eyes open and were starting to nod off in mid-sentence.

"Okay, time for bed. We can talk again in the morning. Molly, you should get going too, before your folks come looking for you," his mother ordered.

Molly said good night and headed to her apartment, promising to come back in a few hours. Mathew said good night and closed the door. Dillon hit the couch and fell asleep instantly.

Turning around Mathew saw his mother leaning against the kitchen door, looking at him, tears in her eyes. Making his way to his room, Mathew apologized for the hundredth time. "Sorry for making you worry, Mom. I didn't mean to. The situation got so out of control, I got caught up in it and couldn't find my way back home."

"Don't worry, honey. I'm just glad you're safe. Now get some sleep," she said, kissing him on top of the head, as he leaned over to take off his shoes. She gently urged him toward his room. Although she put on a brave façade, she was unable to hide her concern about the congealed blood on his clothes and in his hair.

CHAPTER 13

• • •

"DISOBEDIENCE WILL BE PUNISHED! DISOBEDIENCE will be punished!" This was what Mathew woke up to the next day. Near the harbor he saw smoke and fires beneath the scorching sun. They had to get a move on, but first he needed a real shower. He stunk so bad, he was holding his own breath. After spending more time in the shower than he ever had, he got dressed and headed to the kitchen. There he found his mother, Dillon and Molly talking at the kitchen table. An empty plate sat in front of Dillon. No matter how much he shoved down his gullet, he was always hungry. It was like his throat and stomach didn't connect.

"What'd you want? I'm a growing boy," he said reading Mathew's thoughts. This got strange looks from his mother and Molly who didn't understand his comment or who it was directed toward.

"Hi, Mathew!" Molly said.

"Morning, honey, or should I say good afternoon. Let me get you some food," his mother added.

"Hi, Mathew!" Dillon said mimicking Molly and scoring a point.

His mom and Molly went on talking, while Dillon made kissy faces when they weren't watching. He's lucky he's on the other side of the table, Mathew thought as he started stuffing food down his throat. I swear I'm going to make him pay.

"Hurry up, dude. We got to go," Dillon said back in serious mode, getting up from the table and looking for his sneakers. "Where'd I put those shoes?" he asked out loud.

"Go where?" his mom and Molly asked at the same time.

"Back to the rebel army, Mom. We told you last night. We're on a mission for the Colonel," Mathew said between bites.

"Honey, you two have done enough. You aren't going anywhere. We will get someone else to deliver your message."

"No, Mom. We need to do this. First of all, we don't know who to trust and second Dillon and I are the only ones who know where the rebels are."

"But, Mathew--"

"We'll be careful, I promise. If we don't get the information to the rebels, they won't stand a chance against the aliens. It's time we did something. Enough is enough. They invaded our country, they destroyed our way of life, they've killed millions of innocent people, and they continue to demean and brutalize us. We have to stand up to them! It's time we take the war to them!" Mathew's passion left his mom dumbfounded. "You know Dad would agree with me, if he were still alive. Freedom and liberty have a price. Well, I'm about to pay for our portion."

In tears she hugged her son tightly. All she said was, "My little boy is growing up. I'm proud of you. Your dad is proud of you. Just promise me you'll be careful."

"Promise," Mathew said, embarrassed to see tears in Molly's eyes, too. Dillon wore a big, fat smile. "What?" Mathew asked.

"Who's Rambo now?" Dillon asked, clearly proud of his friend. "Mrs. Holloway, if he was any older, that son of yours would get elected president with that speech." "And Molly would be your first lady," he whispered so only his friend heard him. He faked notching another point on his card, with his finger in the air.

Ignoring him, his face red, Mathew finishing eating his meal. Once done, he reviewed their plans with Dillon. His mom and Molly sat and listened, adding advice or suggestions wherever possible. After putting their weapons and some other things into a backpack, they were ready to set off.

Hugging his mom tightly, he promised to be careful and come back as soon as he could. With tears in her eyes she kissed him on the forehead and wished him luck. As she turned her attention to Dillon, who had just finished saying his good-byes to Molly, Mathew found himself alone with Molly.

"Please be safe. I'll miss you," she said as she gave him a hug and a quick kiss on the lips before anyone could see. As they broke apart, Mathew found that he was having a hard time not smiling. Not wanting his mom to think he was happy leaving and definitely not wanting to give any more ammunition to Dillon, he kept his face as neutral as possible.

"Let's go," he said as he opened the door, avoiding looking at his mom. He didn't want her tears to be the last thing he saw leaving his home, possibly for the last time. Making their way down the stairs they exited the building through the front door they had recently come through. They left the neighborhood traveling north, hoping to catch a ride once out of the city they. People were going about their business, and nobody paid them any attention. Even the patrols had decreased. Maybe we will be lucky and get out of the city unnoticed thought Mathew as they came around the corner. They were almost to the expressways that led to New Hampshire when the unthinkable happened.

Before Mathew had the slightest warning, his arms were locked to his sides by a large metal band. It had materialized around his chest, pinning his arms to his sides as if by magic. He felt himself lifted straight off the ground. Mathew increased his struggles trying to get free, but to no avail. Whoever was holding him was much stronger and taller than him, since his feet were dangling in the air. He tried to twist around to see who had hold of him.

"Aliens!" cried Dillon.

"Run Dillon! Run," he urged, still struggling to free himself.

"What about you?" Dillon asked as he struggled with his own alien. Suddenly a shot rang out, and the alien Dillon was engaged with crumbled to the ground. Mathew was flung about as if he were a rag doll. Dillon was standing there, the alien's weapon in his hands. In the struggle, he must have gotten hold of the Magar soldier's gun and used it to defend himself.

As his own attacker screamed in his ear, Mathew shouted, "RUN, RUN! Get away from here."

Dillon just stood there, pointing the alien weapon at Mathew's attacker. It was a Mexican standoff. Mathew's attacker had his hands full holding Mathew up in the air, prohibiting him from grabbing his own weapon without dropping him. But if he dropped him to grab his gun, Dillon would shoot him. Dillon couldn't shoot for fear of hitting his friend. So the alien soldier was currently using Mathew as a shield, while Dillon stood there, pointing his newly acquired alien plasma gun. Mathew found himself envious of his friend's new toy. Always the lucky one, he thought, momentarily forgetting that he was in the embrace of a very ugly and smelly alien creature with horrendous breath.

"What'd we do, Mathew?"

"Run! Don't worry about me. Just get away. I'll catch up to you later if I can. Just go," Mathew yelled

"Are you sure? I can't just leave you."

"I'm sure, and, yes, you can. Remember why we are doing this," Mathew said cryptically so as not to give anything away. Seeing their mission register on his friend's face, Mathew knew that Dillon understood his message.

"Okay then, good luck," his friend said. "Just don't get killed, because your mom will crucify me, not to mention what your girlfriend will do to me."

"She's not my girlfriend!"

Dillon hesitated another second as they silently said their good-byes, wondering if they'd ever see each other again. Reaching down while still pointing his weapon in their direction, Dillon grabbed the fallen backpack. Hoisting it onto his shoulder, he turned and fled.

"Get off me! Let me go," Mathew yelled at his captor, fighting to break free. "And haven't you ever heard of a toothbrush? Your breath stinks worse than a backed-up port-a-potty. I guess you're not big on oral healthcare where you come from, huh? If you want, I've got a name of a good dentist. Clean you right up. Bet you even get a prize for a being a good boy if you behave and open wide."

"Quiet, human. Don't move. Do not annoy me any further," growled the alien soldier, exposing several rows of extremely sharp jagged teeth encrusted with food particles and loads of plaque and tartar that would have put any self-respecting dental hygienist either in her special happy place or early retirement.

"Or what, huh? You going to kill me? I'm not scared of you!"

"Silence, you belligerent pup," barked the alien before punching him in the back of the head and rendering him unconscious.

CHAPTER 14

• • •

DILLON HAD TAKEN OFF AT a run, trying to gain as much distance as possible before more alien soldiers were called into the area to find and apprehend him. He had to get the information about the weapons caravan to the Colonel as quickly as possible. He knew his mission took priority, but he couldn't get Mathew out of his mind. Even though Mathew had urged him to escape and carry on with their assignment, Dillon couldn't abandon his friend, no matter what.

Instead of heading north like they had discussed, he changed direction and made his way back into the city. It took him quite a long time to return, since he had to keep hiding from the alien patrols. When he finally made it back, it was nighttime. He hid out in a destroyed building after making sure it wasn't occupied. That was the bad thing with the majority of the city destroyed; survivors were setting up house anywhere they could find. Making his way through the rubble he found a spot behind a large concrete slab where he could bed down for the night. He felt safe knowing he would be protected by the elements as well as prying eyes. He made himself comfortable, using his backpack as a pillow. He placed his weapon beside him, just in case. As he lay there, he thought about Mathew.

He was proud of his friend for the courage and patriotism he had displayed, but he knew that he was going back. Mathew had been his best friend since they were little, and he knew that Mathew would come after him if the situation were reversed. He had proved his loyalty at the Battle of Charlestown, when he had stayed by his side. His friend had been through so much over the past year, least of which was getting shot. Dillon didn't know what he would have done if his father had been killed. Even though he had lost many friends and relatives it must have been horrible to lose a parent. Mathew had not only persevered but he had gotten stronger, for himself and for his mother.

Through the years they had become more like brothers than friends. They had spent so much time together, they knew what the other was thinking, they were so close. They could communicate without speaking. They enjoyed one-upping each other more for entertainment than competition. They had gone hiking and camping together. Their families had spent holidays together. He had spent more time at Mathew's house than he had his own. They watched each other's backs and had backed up each other countless times in schoolyard and playground fights. When one day they had come out on the losing end of a particularly nasty brawl, they had signed up for karate classes together. Going through the vigorous training and examination process they got their black belts on the same day years later.

His mind wandering as it slipped out of conscientiousness and into sleep, he smiled at the memory of a particularly funny incident involving a neighborhood bully. They both hated bullies and caused them tremendous amounts of grief over the years as payback for their reprehensible actions. This one incident took place on a neighborhood playground when they were twelve years old.

Like any other Saturday morning they had gone to the park to shoot hoops on the basketball courts. While playing a game of horse they noticed a small boy in a wheelchair watching from the sidelines. Without even discussing it, they both approached the boy, introducing themselves, and asked if he wanted to join them.

"Hi, my name is Mathew, and my stinky friend here is Dillon. We were wondering if you want to join us. I'm tired of winning all the time," Mathew said, razzing his friend. Although Dillon was a decent enough player, he had been losing horribly all day.

"Hey! I'm just having an off day," he said, pushing Mathew.

"I'm Jason." The boy laughed. "I'm okay just watching you guys play."

At first the boy refused, telling them that he wasn't any good and didn't want to interrupt their game. The boys sensing his true desire to play gently coaxed him into changing his mind. The three then proceeded onto the court and commenced playing. They took turns calling their shots and shooting the necessary baskets to win the game. Even though Jason was in a wheelchair he made more shots than he missed, the difference being that he wheeled himself to the necessary spots instead of walking. As the game progressed, they gained an audience of kids, mostly their age or younger, that watched and rooted for their favorite player and jeered his opponents. Some of the kids went to their school; others were just kids from the neighborhood. Most knew Mathew and Dillon and how competitive they were, so they were enjoying the show and all the smack talk. Jason also garnered several fans that encouraged and supported him, especially when he made shots the two friends missed. It was all in good fun, everybody having a great time until one of the spectators started making disparaging rude comments toward Jason.

"Hey, speedy, how about trying a jumper," he taunted. "Be careful you don't run over anyone's toes."

He was sitting on his bicycle, a soda can in his hand yelling and insulting the boy for no reason. He was a large kid more fat than muscle, his belly bulging under his too-tight tee-shirt. Oily, unwashed hair falling into his beady little eyes, he was constantly tossing his head back and forth to see. A cruel mouth with a broken front tooth and an acne problem completed the picture. Because he was bigger than anyone there, the audience soon moved away, not wanting to get caught up in something that didn't concern them. The three boys on the court did their best to ignore him, but he kept at it, goading them on, looking for a fight. Mathew and Dillon having learned patience, discipline and self-control under the tutelage of Sensei Hunn continued to ignore his remarks. Jason on the other hand got more and more uncomfortable and eventually decided to leave the court. Mathew tried to talk him into staying and finishing the game, but failed. The situation had gotten too prickly and personal for him and he eventually took his leave, wheeling himself off the court in the opposite direction of the bully. The boys watched him as he made his way out of the park heading home dejected and hurt from the constant barrage of discouraging remarks and insults. By this time Mathew was fuming, barely holding it together. Dillon, knowing how his friend felt about bullies turned in his direction hoping to placate him.

"I swear, I'm going to give that guy a piece of my mind," Mathew said, turning in the direction of the bully, finally unable to restrain himself any longer.

Dillon looking to intercede, tried to stop his friend from causing an altercation, but when he turned around, he noticed the guy on the bike was gone. Perplexed, he scanned the park, trying to determine his whereabouts. Unable to find him he turned to his friend, only to find him missing as well. Looking in the direction Jason had gone once again, he saw Mathew running toward him, but he was too late. The damage had been done.

Dillon witnessed the scene in its entirety. The tyrant on the bike had left the park and followed the boy in the wheelchair out onto the sidewalk and had stopped in front of him blocking his way. Even though he couldn't hear what was said, Dillon saw him reach over and empty his can of soda over the boys head. Dropping the empty can he then flipped the boy and his chair over, spilling them onto the sidewalk. Looking up, the bully noticed Mathew running toward him. Smiling and giving him the one finger salute, he turned his bike around and rode off laughing maniacally over his shoulder.

Mathew reached the downed boy a few seconds later only to find him crying. The fall had broken his arm. By then other people had noticed the fallen boy and run over to help. Someone called an ambulance and the boy was taken to the hospital. Having run up himself, Dillon heard someone say that he knew where Jason lived and he was going to go notify his parents. As the crowd dispersed, the boys went home.

"We have to do something," Mathew fumed. "He can't get away with it, I won't let him. When I see that guy again, I'm going to beat him senseless."

"I agree someone has to teach that guy a lesson. What he did was not only wrong, but evil."

The rest of the day was spent planning their revenge. It was finalized over the phone that night and put into effect a week later. It was one of their better bully-busting achievements, of which there were many over the years.

Asking around the neighborhood they found out that the bully's name was Greg Watkins and he lived off Hanover Street. Taking turns the boys followed him around all week trying to learn his routine. They found out that every day around four o'clock he rode his bike to a corner convenience store and after locking it to a street-light he entered and played an old stand-up Pac-Man video machine, while stuffing his face with Ho-Hos and Ring-Dings. He spent about an hour feeding quarters into the machine and breaking a sweat trying to beat one of the easiest games ever invented. Not only did he waste his money playing a game he would never master, but he also stuffed enough junk food down his throat to maintain his pimply complexion for years to come. Finalizing their plan Friday night, they put it into effect the next day.

When Greg entered the store on Saturday, the boys were waiting around the corner. As Dillon kept an eye on their target, Mathew removed a small handsaw that he had borrowed from Mr. Marks from his backpack and approached the bully's bicycle. Gently, but quickly he sawed through the spokes of the bicycle's wheels leaving the tiniest of attachments on each one. He was just finish-ing, when Dillon ran over and told him that their victim was on his way. Climbing on their bikes and donning ski masks to hide their identity, the boys waited for the bully to exit the store. They had positioned themselves about ten feet away from his bicycle and armed themselves with six eggs a piece also taken from Mathew's backpack, com-pliments of his parents' refrigerator. They watched as Greg undid his lock and climbed aboard his bike, ready to ride away.

"Hey, Dufus," Mathew yelled as he hurled egg after egg in his direction, scoring multiple hits.

"Yeah, loser! Here, have some more," Dillon added as he released his own eggs, several of which hit the bully in the head and face.

"I'm going to kill you," screamed the yolk-dripping tyrant, trying to clean his eyes from the gelatinous mess.

The boys turned their bikes and took off, hoping and praying he would follow. Angry, screaming obscenities that would put a sailor to shame, he took off after them pedaling as fast as he could. Not wanting to lose him the boys slowed down. Thinking that he was gaining ground, he pedaled even harder to catch up. All of a sudden, Greg's wheels collapsed, his forward momentum halted, his bicycle crumbling like a house of cards as the front fork jammed into the pavement sending him flying over his handle bars. He landed face first into a pile of trash waiting to be picked up by the sanitation department. To add insult to injury the trash was primarily comprised of spoiled fish and baby diapers. Sprawled out, garbage sticking to his clothes and a dirty diaper plastered to his egg washed head, he laid there stunned and bruised. Watching for a few minutes longer, enjoying the fruits of their labor, as the bully rolled around trying to extricate himself from the pile of smelly trash, the boys took their leave.

"Serves him right," Mathew said to Dillon as they rode away. Another successful mission by the bully patrol, they both thought as they pedaled their bikes home.

So there was no way he was going to leave Mathew behind. Before falling asleep he prayed that his friend was alright.

The next morning found Dillon walking the streets trying to hear news of his friend. He asked around trying to ascertain any helpful information. He had to be careful who he asked questions, since there were many alien spies and sympathizers around willing to sell him down the river for some money or extra food. Others just wanted to take focus away from their activities by directing the aliens elsewhere. He walked the city for two days trying to find his friend, eating anything he could find and sleeping anywhere he deemed safe. He spent more time dodging alien patrols than anything else, not wanting to take a chance on them recognizing him. He had seen several posters with his likeness offering a reward for information leading to his whereabouts and capture. Even though the drawings on the posters were vague, Dillon knew it was him in the picture. For that reason he wore an old baseball cap he had found in a trash heap, hoping to avoid being recognized.

It was towards the end of the second day, when he was told of the alien headquarters in the old Bank of America building. A little old lady pushing a cart filled with all her belongings offered the information as they sat next to each other in a park. Feeling sorry for her he shared a bag of potato chips he had found in a destroyed market, the previous day, while listening to her story about losing her whole family during the raid. She was out visiting a friend when the attack began and when she eventually returned home, she found the whole building had collapsed, trapping and killing her husband, daughter, and grandchild.

He listened quietly as she shared her memories. She was heartbroken, homeless and alone. Her story sad, her future unsure, but not unique, since few were not affected in the same way, suffering just as much if not more. These were difficult times for all, but hopefully one day they would be able to rebuild, mentally, emotionally, and physically. Wishing her luck, he bade her farewell as he continued his search.

With nothing better to do, since he had exhausted all his ideas, he made his way in the direction of the alien headquarters hoping to have better luck than his aimless wandering had produced so far. It was almost sundown when he saw the distinctive building in front of him. One of the few left standing unscathed it dominated the street. The area was teeming with aliens and humans. This was the busiest part of the city. He thought he could blend in without arousing suspicion. He spent the rest of the evening walking up and down the street trying to see if there was a way in. He had seen many humans had entering and exiting the building. They must be work crews as well as sympathizers he thought to himself as he watched the flow of people. He left the area later that evening to avoid suspicion when the throng of pedestrians decreased for the night.

The next morning found him leaning against a building farther up the road; chewing on a protein bar and drinking from a bottle of water he had filled several streets over from a communal hose. He noticed a difference in the activity than the day before. It seemed to be more frantic. Sensing something was about to happen he maintained his position and waited. Around noon he saw the Supreme Commander arrive with his entourage and Mathew in tow.

CHAPTER 15

• • •

MATHEW WOKE UP LYING ON a cold metal floor in the dark. Still groggy and unable to focus, he felt as if he were floating in a dream. He heard voices but they were too far off to make out what was said. He heard other sounds and felt a dull throbbing throughout his body... "Oh my God, I'm on one of their spaceships," he thought. He suddenly felt himself lifted off the floor, tossed through the air and then slammed back down with bone jarring force. He saw a bright white light before he passed out again.

Later, he was awakened by more clanking, thumping, and rattling noises. Trying to focus and clear the fog from his mind, he attempted to sit up. More noises and rumbles permeated his senses. What? Huh? What's going on? After a few minutes of wildly grasping for some tendrils of cognitive ability, he thought, we must be in the air. More excited than frightened, he finally managed to sit up.

His head was spinning. His stomach gave a queer lift and heave, confirming his suspicions of flying. As the last layers of fog cleared his brain, the enormity of his situation became clear. He was a prisoner on an alien spaceship. He would more than likely be tortured for information and then killed. He had to find a way out.

His head felt as if it were going to explode. Either he had hurt it again when it had smacked into the bulkhead, or that alien didn't hold back when he knocked him out the first time. Creeping to his feet he felt the floor tilt beneath him. He reached out to balance himself and found a wall to his left. Moving closer to the wall he made his way clockwise trying to get an idea of the size and shape of the room. It seemed like a round room with smooth metal walls. He was about to try crossing the room when all lights went on and he saw an alien standing ten feet away, a snarl on his face. He was pointing a gun at him.

"Come now," he ordered in that annoying guttural style.

Shocked, Mathew blinked his eyes to adjust to the sudden brightness. "Where are you taking me?" he asked. Looking around he realized he had been correct. He was in a round room with smooth metal walls. There was a metal bench bolted to the floor in the center of the room. He laughed to himself, realizing that he would have run into it if he had traversed the room. At least the alien's sudden appearance saved him from bruising his shins.

The alien didn't take his eyes off him, but Mathew noticed his finger moving toward the trigger. "The Supreme Commander wants to see you. MOVE IT!"

Not wanting to push his luck he sort of floated toward his captor. Must be some sort of anti-gravitational pull or something he thought. The big alien grabbed him by the scruff of his neck and pushed him forward into a passageway.

"Easy there, big boy. There's no need to get rough. Didn't your mama teach you any manners?" he said using his best Mr. Marks impression. The old guy was always harping on how rude the younger generation was. So why not honor him by insulting the big bag of manure currently in charge of his well-being.

"Move," the soldier growled, shoving him in the back with the muzzle of his weapon.

A few minutes and a couple more pushes later they entered what looked to Mathew like the control room. He saw several other aliens sitting or standing at different stations. Looking out a large window, he realized that they were in space. Seeing the Earth rotating in the distance, he was shocked and excited at the same time. No one was going to believe him. Dillon would be so jealous that he'd drop a load in his pants. That's if Mathew survived long enough to rub it in his face.

Here he was about to face the leader of the alien invasion. He didn't know what to expect and to say he was scared would be a monumental understatement.

"Come here, human," said a voice from his right.

Mathew froze. He was facing the alien supreme commander, General Moutari. He stood and stared mouth agape at the general. His excitement replaced with fear, he found himself glued to the floor.

"I said, COME HERE!" yelled the General. "Are you stupid? Did you not hear me?"

"I'm a, a sorry, sir," he said as he finally felt his feet moving.

"You will answer my questions, or I will shoot you into space through one of our torpedo tubes. Do you understand?"

"Y-yes sir."

"I want to know where the rebel hideout is."

"I-I don't know what you're talking about. I'm just a kid," he tried.

"Do not lie to me! You were caught running from our patrols. Where were you heading," he demanded.

In that pivotal moment, gripped by fear and apprehension, Mathew made his decision. As if some divine power had suddenly filled him with courage he decided to not give them any information, no matter what they did to him. He was angry. He was angry at himself for getting caught. He was angry that his mom was worried about him. He was angry at the aliens for invading his country and ruining their lives. But more importantly he was angry that they had killed all those people and especially his father. No matter what, he wasn't going to say a word even at the cost of his life. But he would escape; he told himself, if the opportunity arose, so he could continue the fight.

While Mathew pleaded his innocence and made his resolution, an alien ran over to the general and spoke to him in their language. The General stared at the Earth while the crew stood about tensely waiting for his orders.

"Head back to Boston," he growled. "And throw that brat back in his cell until I figure out what to do with him."

A guard grabbed Mathew from behind and forced him from the room. He was half pushed half dragged back to his cell. The door opened as if by magic and he was unceremoniously thrown inside. Before he could regain his feet, the door slammed shut and he was left alone.

Mathew felt the ship increase speed. Probably just entered the Earth's gravitational pull, he thought. He couldn't help smiling, wondering what his mom would say if she knew he had actually learned something from playing all those video games. The one good that came out of his little conversation with the General was that they had left the lights on in his cell. Too bad there wasn't anything to use as a weapon or tool to open the door. He sat down and thought over his predicament. Even if he could escape his prison, what was he to do? He couldn't get off the alien spacecraft or fight for control of the ship. Besides being seriously outnumbered, he didn't know how to fly the alien craft. With the way his luck was going lately he'd probably send the ship to Pluto. He was having a hard enough time understanding Magarnese, he couldn't deal with having to learn Doganese as well. How come I come up with this stuff when I'm by myself and there's no one else to appreciate my comedic talent? Pluto...Doganese... Priceless!

The alien spaceship shuddered as if a major gale of wind had accosted it. The sudden turbulence caused Mathew's stomach to flip and he felt lightheaded. He put his head between his legs, trying to steady his breathing. It was a good thing he hadn't eaten in a while or else he would have already tossed his cookies. He heard shouts and what he assumed were orders echoing throughout the ship. By the level of noise and activity, he assumed they were getting ready to land in Boston.

In a few minutes the turbulence slackened, but the noise level increased. It seemed that hundreds of aliens were moving throughout the ship. Mathew shivered in his cell, wondering what was to become of him. The General was a mystery Mathew thought. Clearly he wanted something from me, I mean why else was he still alive? Perhaps he wanted to torture him or turn him against the rebels. Lately the rebels were becoming more and more active, causing more havoc and damage to the Magar forces. Although small in scale, they had to be worrying the alien invaders, who had increased their patrols ten-fold. With nothing left for him to do, Mathew waited for the spaceship to land.

An hour or so later, Mathew was once again removed from his cell. This time he had two guards, not one. They were just as pleasant as his first one. With nothing to lose he started asking questions hoping to glean information that might come in useful. No matter what he tried, he got absolutely nothing other than a love tap to his already pounding head by one of his guards. The guards only talked among themselves in their language.

At last, they stopped at a door at to the end of a corridor. Mathew was about to make another comment that would have probably earned him another smack in the head when the door opened and he was shoved forward.

"Well human, are you ready to answer my questions?" rumbled the alien commander without turning away from a computer display.

Mathew remained silent, taking a closer look at the General. The guy was enormous. Close to seven feet tall, he was heavily muscled, his body chiseled as if made of granite. His shoulders had the wingspan of a small jet; his hands were the size of serving platters. Covered in scaly black skin, he sported a huge head dominated by a sharply sloped forehead, dead recessed eyes and a boxer's flat nose. All this was nestled below a forest of brillo-like hair that was standing straight up, all balanced on a neck so wide it would make a sumo wrestler's thigh look small. Finally, a large, cruel mouth with razor-sharp teeth and a lantern jaw completed the picture. The guy looked like the demon spawn child of the old Alien versus Predators movies.

The alien chuckled menacingly. "You're a tough one," he said, a hint of praise in his voice. "I like that. You are my prisoner and you will obey my orders. If you do not I will punish you severely. I am not very patient, human. You will tell me what I need to know."

"I don't have anything to say," he heard himself utter.

"I bet you don't. I will not tolerate any disobedience or dissent. Do you understand me!" The General's voice rose in volume as his anger took over. "You rebels will be punished and made an example of. When we are done with you, the rest of the filthy humans will never question our authority again. We took over your little world as we have multiple others. You now serve us. We are your new masters."

"Bite me, you piece of alien scum!" Mathew yelled. Without thinking he rushed the General. Suddenly, he felt himself sail across the room. As he hit the floor he realized the General had swatted him like a fly. He hadn't even gotten a hand on him. Getting up from the floor he looked back defiantly readying himself for another attempt. The alien commander could squash him like a bug, but he didn't care.

"I know you have the information I need, human. I feel it in my bones. You will give it to me or the previous slap will seem as if you were hit by a feather. You are a rebel and you will yield to my demands," he growled. "You will rot in your cell if you defy me."

"Do whatever you want, you freak. I told you, I don't know anything and even if I did, I still wouldn't tell you, just on general principles," cried Mathew as he struggled against the two Magar soldiers who held him.

"Maybe you will and maybe you won't. Either way, you will suffer," he said. "Get this insolent pup out of my sight. I will deal with him later. Put him back in his cell. Oh, and by the way, we have your friend, just in case you thought he got away," he said with a vicious laugh.

Mathew winced as once again he was pushed from behind and sent stumbling back toward his cell. Had the aliens captured Dillon? Was he a prisoner too? In any case, Mathew wasn't going to say anything about the rebels or the plot to attack the weapons convoy. He had to find a way off this ship. As he was pushed by a window he saw that the ship had once again landed in Boston harbor. At least he was back home, sort of.

Once back in his cell he promptly sat on the floor with his back against the bulkhead. Trying to think his way out exhausted him and he must have fallen asleep. Unexpectedly, a swift kick woke him up. He was quite impressed with himself when he noticed three guards instead of his usual two. They must really be afraid of me, the Great Alien Killer, he laughed to himself.

"What?" he asked sleepily. "Is there a Three Stooges convention going on?"

"The General wants you," said one of the guards.

Unable to resist and with nothing better to do, he got up and walked out of his cell. Moe, Larry, and Curly followed close behind, occasionally pushing him in the necessary direction, as they talked among themselves.

As they entered the ship's command center, the General was surrounded by his elite troops getting ready to depart. "Are we going on a picnic?" Mathew asked. Wow, those blows to my head must have activated my wise-ass gene, he thought. Again, someone showed him some love from behind. Those love taps were really starting to hurt. He stumbled a few steps forward to the General. Looking up into his dead eyes, Mathew felt true fear. The guy was formidable. He oozed power and malevolence out of every pore. He made the grim reaper look like a choir boy.

"You will come with me, so I can keep an eye on you," he said, cuffing him in the head for effect.

Stumbling forward, he whacked his head against a seat bolted to the floor. He regained his feet, feeling almost giddy from the new head injury. Not being able to help himself, he yelled, "Yes, Mein Fuhrer!" slapping his chest and extending his arm, as he had seen the Nazis do in so many movies about that little psychopath Adolf Hitler.

Before he even had a chance to marvel at his antics, one of the elite troops grabbed him by the arm and pulled him along as they exited the ship. Walking well behind the general and his entourage, Mathew was glad to be on solid ground. It was a relief to see Boston again. He saw several more alien ships than usual. "Where are we going?" he tried, not really expecting an answer. He noticed that the General was shielded by his private troops. I guess even he is afraid of a sniper putting a bullet in his head. They moved quickly, making good time. They avoided the most damaged streets but still had to skirt some rough patches before making it to their destination, the financial district. Aliens and humans were staring at him. The aliens were smirking and gesturing, while the humans avoided making eye contact, hence they be accused of corroboration. Both groups knew Mathew's fate.

• • •

CHAPTER 16

THEY ENTERED THE BANK OF America on Washington Street. This must be one of the aliens' ground command headquarters, Mathew thought. The place was packed with aliens of all shapes and sizes. He even saw aliens not belonging to the Magar race. They all stopped what they were doing and moved out of the way so the general and his group could pass. They bowed their heads, showing the Supreme Commander the necessary respect and admiration his alien ego demanded. Looking at all the different aliens, Mathew momentarily forgot his perilous predicament. He was brought back to reality when he received another shot to the back of the head. Not having the energy or inclination to respond he just shuffled forward, trying to buy some time to further scope out the situation.

Not knowing what to expect, he feverishly tried to find a way to escape. He was caught off guard when he was suddenly thrust into to a hall closet and the door was slammed and the lock clicked. He rattled the knob with no effect. Kicking the steel-plated base only hurt his foot and feeling around the perimeter only proved that the hardware was all on the outside. The door was closed tighter than the vault door at Fort Knox. Helpless, he sat down and waited. A small trickle of light seeped through the crack at the bottom of the door as his own sweat trickled into his eyes. Dropping down with his cheek to the floor he tried to look through the crack. All he saw were feet walking by and all he got for his trouble was dirt in his eye. Sitting up and rubbing his eye, he repositioned himself. The floor creaked as he made himself comfortable. He had a feeling he would be there for a while.

It must have been hours later when he heard the knob rattle. Maybe they were making sure the door is still locked he thought, as he tried to wake up.

All of a sudden, he heard a whisper. "Mathew, Mathew." The heat must be getting to me, he thought. That sounded like Dillon.

"Mathew, are you in there? Come on, dude, answer me!" he said more loudly.

"Dillon, is that you?" Mathew queried, rubbing the sleep from his eyes.

"Yeah, bro, it's me. Time to go," Dillon answered as he turned the key and unlocked the door. Mathew hurled himself at him, hugging him tightly. Dillon returned the hug, happy his friend was still alive. Realizing what they were doing, they quickly broke apart.

"Stop being such a girl," Dillon said a smirk on his face. "Come on, we have to get out of here before your guard gets back." Dillon closed and locked the closet door as he guided Mathew down the hall toward the emergency exit.

They were halfway to the exit when the door was flung open and Mathew's guard entered from outside. Seeing his captive free, he let out a bloodcurdling howl and charged down the hall toward the startled boys.

"Uh oh, your buddy's back. Run for it!" Dillon said as he turned and ran back the way they had come. Mathew followed. He spared a moment to look at his jailor who was barreling toward them.

"This way," Dillon yelled as he turned left toward a staircase leading up to the next floor. They charged up the steps two at a time. The stairs led to a large hallway on the second floor. The boys stopped at the landing to catch their breath. The alien was still running after them, even angrier than before. He was taking the steps three at a time. Veins the size of electrical cords had erupted from his neck and he was foaming at the mouth as he yelled at them in his native tongue. The hallway they had entered was full of aliens as well as humans, who still hadn't taken notice of the boys and the ascending alien.

Turning away from their pursuer, they weaved through the hall as quickly as possible. They were running out of time. Once their pursuer made it to the top of the stairs, all hell would break loose. They had to circumnavigate the aliens as well as the people that were coming in and out of offices. A moment later, the alien burst in to the hallway, yelling and pointing in their direction. Everyone froze. Mathew and Dillon increased their speed looking for another way back down to the first floor and freedom.

The alien fired in the direction of the fleeing boys. His shots scattered the onlookers, who dived for cover. The alien took off running down the hall...The boys came to the end of the hall taking a right-hand turn just as another shot rang out. More yelling and screaming meant others had joined the chase. Mathew and Dillon found themselves in an especially long corridor, running the length of the building. With no other choice they raced away from their pursuers.

"There's another stairwell," Mathew said gulping for air, pointing to an exit door halfway down the corridor.

"Where?" Dillon asked out of breath.

"There, by the fire extinguisher."

All of a sudden a door opened at the end of the hall, and a group of alien soldiers came rushing out, no doubt alerted by the noise and an alarm that had just been set off. Mathew figured he and Dillon might be better off turning back and taking their chances with his jailer, his weapon notwithstanding. Dillon did not have such misconceptions and raced toward the exit door. Mathew followed on his heels. It was going to be close. The alien soldiers were closing in from one end, his jailer from another, the only benefit being that they didn't shoot for fear of hitting one another.

Reaching the door moments before the advancing aliens, the boys tried to exit into the stairwell. But the alien guard covered the remaining distance in two apelike bounds and landed in their path. The boys froze, shaken by the sight of the fuming alien. Mathew was surprised his heart didn't stop as the alien backhanded him into the opposing wall. The blow sent shock waves down to his toes as his head slammed into the concrete. Stunned he fell to his knees, tears blurring his vision. Through half-closed lids he saw his jailer advancing, hoping to finish the job his first blow left undone. Angry, hurt, and scared out of his mind, he hurled himself headfirst below the alien's belt. The alien howled and doubled over in pain. Dillon plowed into him knocking the pistol from his grasp and taking him to the floor. Mathew scrambled to his feet and stumbled into the fire extinguisher. He yanked it off its mount and brought it down on the alien's helmet with all his might. The alien was sent crashing smashing his face into the floor. Blood jetted from his nose spraying the wall and floor in a pattern any Impressionist painter would be proud of. Mathew then retrieved the alien's fallen weapon and fired several shots at the advancing alien soldiers. Then the gun jammed and Mathew threw it at them.

"Come on, Mathew," Dillon yelled, his holding the door open. "His friends are almost here," he hollered, trying to make himself heard above the wailing alarm while pointing behind him to the running mass of aliens heading in their direction from the other end of the hall.

Turning around Mathew saw more aliens heading in their direction. Mathew leaped through the open door and Dillon followed, slamming the door behind them.

The boys flung themselves down the stairs at breakneck speed. They dashed onto the darkened street. Mathew realized he'd been in that closet longer than he thought. After what seemed like miles of running, they stopped to catch their breaths. It seemed to Mathew that all he did lately was run and get pummeled.

"What are you doing here? You were supposed to return to the Colonel."

"I know, but I couldn't leave you," his friend said looking over his shoulder to make sure they were safe.

"How'd you find me? How'd you get here? Why? How?" Mathew had so many questions he didn't know where to start.

"Listen, let's get out of town first and I'll tell you everything. When they tell the General that you're gone all hell will break loose and I don't want to be around."

CHAPTER 17

• • •

MATHEW AND DILLON CONTINUED THEIR trek north out of town and were able to hitch a ride with an old lady driving a 1960s pickup truck loaded with shovels, rakes and hoes. They rode in the bed of the truck resting on bags of fertilizer, judging by the smell. The front seat was taken up by the driver and her two very angry looking Rottweilers. The boys were just happy they didn't have to walk. Enjoying the breeze, they silently watched the miles disappear. They made good time and covered a significant distance when they finally had to part ways.

"You boys be safe, you hear!" their driver said as she let them out. The only words she'd spoken other than, "Where you headin'?" when they'd first flagged her down and asked for a ride.

It was well past two in the morning when they came upon a deserted farmhouse and decided to stop for the night. They collapsed on the living room couch. Dillon still carried the backpack from which he removed a couple of protein bars and a bottle of water. Mathew devoured his bar in record time. He had not realized how hungry he was. Taking a sip of water he jealously eyed his friend's bar.

"What, didn't your friends feed you?" Dillon asked as he handed over half of his own. "Half is all you get, so stop with the puppy eyes. I'm not Molly you know," he said, moving quickly out of reach.

Too tired to pummel his friend, Mathew said, "Tell me what happened."

"Well, not much to tell. When I left you, I ran for a mile or so. As I rested, I thought about you and decided I couldn't leave you. So, I made my way back into the city and hid out in an abandoned building until morning. The next morning I made my way down to the financial district. I asked around trying to find where the alien headquarters were. I was told about the Bank of America building, so I figured if you were still alive, that's where you'd be or eventually end up. I waited for three days hovering around their headquarters by day and hiding out at night."

"Wait, three days?" Mathew asked puzzled. "I was gone for three days?"

"Well yeah. Don't you know how long you've been gone?"

"Uh, no, not really. I got hit in the head pretty hard a few times. I must have been unconscious longer than I thought. Well, that explains why I'm so hungry," he said, polishing off the rest of his protein bar. "Go on, tell me what happened next."

"Not much more to tell. I was about to give up, when I saw you go into the building with the General and his entourage. I waited around until I found a way in and saw your guard standing outside the closet. Suspicious as to why he'd be standing outside a closet, I kept myself busy, made it seem as if I belonged there, and when your guard got called away, I tried the door hoping you were in there. The rest as they say is history."

"How'd you know it was a closet he was standing guard at?" Mathew asked marveling at his friend's bravery and perseverance.

"Duuhhh…magic," he said adopting a familiar superior look he was known for. Noticing the look of consternation on Mathew's face, he said, "Dude, chill, there was a sign on the wall next to the door that said CLOSET. Now tell me what happened to you. Did they do freaky experiments on you, where they harvested your 'funny bone' and made you lose your sense of humor or what?"

Not realizing how wired and tightly strung he'd been until that moment, Mathew took in his friend's jibes and tried to relax. "Sorry, dude, just a rough couple of days." Mathew told his story from the moment that they were separated, not leaving out any details.

Dillon was gaping at him. "Wow, you were on an alien spaceship and you mouthed off to the alien commander."

"Yeah, that was pretty stupid, I have to admit. I have the lumps and bruises to prove it."

"Yeah, but how many people can say they did what you did and lived to tell the tale?" his friend said a new respect in his eyes.

Feeling uncomfortable, Mathew thanked his friend for coming back for him. "I'll never forget what you did, Dillon," he said, his eyes suddenly moist.

"You'd do the same for me," Dillon said, just as uncomfortable. "If we don't look out for each other who will?"

Silence followed and then Dillon joked the moment off. "Okay, stop being a girl again and let's figure out our next move. There's no way we can continue on this road. Pretty soon the whole area will be crawling with aliens."

"I know, but what can we do?"

They pondered the matter. Pretty soon exhaustion set in and the boys fell asleep. When they woke up, the sun was rising. They'd finished the last of the protein bars, and again wondered what to do.

Suddenly, Mathew said, "Dillon, the ocean! We can head toward the sea and take a boat along the coast toward New Hampshire. Maybe we can get a fisherman to take us or maybe we can find a boat and sail it ourselves."

"Do you think we can sail ourselves?" Dillon asked.

"I think so. I used to go sailing with my dad all the time. Plus we'll keep close to shore, so we don't get lost," Mathew said liking the idea more and more. Reaching in to the backpack he pulled out the map Colonel Thomas had given them. Even though there were no markings, he knew approximately where the rebel camp was in relation to the coastline. Estimating where they were was a bit harder but after discussing it with Dillon and reviewing some of the local area landmarks, Mathew was pretty sure he knew where they were. After planning the next stage of their journey, then foraged for more food and refilled their water bottles.

"Okay, let's do it. It's not like I have any better ideas," Dillon said. "All this planning is giving me a headache."

Heading toward the coast, they had to hide to avoid roaming alien patrols. It seemed Mathew's absence and capture had taken priority, since they encountered more aliens than was normal for this remote area. By the time they made it to the coast it was dark. With the rising moon lighting the rocky shore, they searched for any fishing vessels anchored close to the area. They were about to run out of seashore, when they came upon an abandoned boat.

"It's too late to see if she's seaworthy. How about we crash here for tonight and check her out in the morning?" Mathew said, walking around the vessel inspecting it for any obvious damage.

"Works for me. I'm beat," Dillon said, dropping to the sand and resting his head against the boat. "Hey, Mathew, I've been meaning to compliment you on your new fighting technique," his friend said unsuccessfully hiding his grin.

Knowing he was walking into a trap, Mathew couldn't help himself. "What new fighting technique?"

"You know. That new style you used to take down that alien guard. I've never seen anyone use his head in that manner in a fight to the death. But who would have guessed that aliens had a weak spot similar to ours? You're the man."

Too embarrassed to even try a witty retort, Mathew just kicked sand at his friend, who continued to laugh harder at his reaction. Ignoring him, Mathew walked to the water to survey the ocean for alien patrols. Nothing, thank God. Returning to the boat he found Dillon fast asleep.

He circled the boat several times and, not finding anything obvious to alarm him, he nudged his sleeping friend. "Hey, get up. We should climb into to the boat and lie down. This way if any patrols happen upon the beach they won't notice us right away."

Too tired to argue, the boys climbed in and fell into a dreamless sleep. The only sounds were the crashing waves against the shore and the growling of their empty stomachs.

The next morning found the boys walking around the boat. Mathew was happy to see it was a sloop--the most common sailboat on the water. He had sailed several with his father over the years. This particular one had a mast, a mainsail, and a foresail. This simple configuration allowed for easy handling and was very efficient for sailing into the wind. The mainsail was already attached to the mast and the boom. This allowed the sail to swing across the boat, depending on the direction of the wind. The foresail was called a jib. This particular boat was called a day-sailor. These types were very useful as personal boats for short journeys. They didn't have large holds, but could easily carry smaller items like fish and tools. They could sustain a speed of about fifteen miles per hour in low winds, making them "all-round" very good travel boats.

It was an old sailboat; similar to one Mathew had sailed with his dad. It looked to be in good condition without any obvious damage. It definitely needed a paint job and the bottom needed to be scraped to remove all the barnacles and dead sea life. The sails were stored beneath deck and looked to be in decent condition if slightly worn and torn. All the equipment necessary to sail her seemed to be aboard. In an old toolbox, Mathew discovered a compass that still worked. "This will come in handy," he said, showing his find.

"I wonder how she got to be here." Dillon wondered out loud as he stood admiring her sleek lines and fast race design.

"She was probably docked and came loose from her mooring during the attack. She probably floated around for a while and eventually she washed up on shore. Judging by the sand and bird droppings, she's been here for months," Mathew said running his finger along the hull and grimacing in disgust.

"Do you think we can get her into the water," Dillon asked.

"Well...I saw some rope in the storage locker. We can tie it to the bow ring and wait for high tide. When the water comes, you push and I'll pull to try to get her floating. What we should do is bring the sail up and hook it up to the mast, that way we'll be ready.

"What time is high tide," Dillon asked as they finished securing the sail. It was hot and heavy work trying to bring up all that dead weight through the small hatch opening but both boys were big and strong for their age. All that running around, doing sports and karate paying off.

"Probably around noon, I think, but I'm not familiar with the tide patterns in this area. What we should do in the meantime is remove as much sand from around her hull as we can, so we can move her when the time comes," Mathew replied not looking forward to more back-breaking work.

"Good idea, we should look for something that we can use to help remove the sand. We should also see what other equipment is available. Maybe we can use some of it when we get her in the water," Dillon agreed. "Sure could use some gloves, my hands are killing me. I have blisters bigger than my toes."

After removing as much sand as they could, they collected everything they found that might be useful during the upcoming trip, a compass being their best find. Done, they sat against the boat and waited for the tide to come in. With the sun shining down on them and the soft sounds of the ocean washing over them, they soon dozed off. Pretty soon both were in dreamland.

Dillon dreamt of food while Mathew dreamt of Molly and her kiss. Late morning turned into early afternoon, and clouds replaced the sun. The wind picked up and the weather turned unseasonably chilly. A light rain started to fall and the tide made its appearance on shore.

• • •

"Dillon, wake up!" Mathew yelled as he was woken by the ocean water soaking his legs. "We have to get moving. Hurry!"

As Dillon came fully awake, he saw his friend pulling on the rope, trying to move the boat farther into the ocean. Taking his place behind the boat he started to push with all his strength. After what seemed like a long time he felt the boat nudge forward.

"It's moving, Mathew!" he yelled to his friend who was suddenly up to his knees in the water. "Keep pulling," he yelled momentarily forgetting that pain in his hands as his blisters burst one by one.

Slowly, pushing, pulling, swearing, and praying, they got the boat in the water. The weather had worsened, and the sea had suddenly gotten wild. The waves had increased in size and frequency, tossing the boat back and forth. Battered and bruised, they maneuvered the boat beyond the breaking surf.

"Quick—jump in. We need to get the sail up," Mathew hollered from the front of the boat, as he moved out of the way to avoid being crushed.

As they made their way over the sides, they were helped as much as hindered by the wild tossing. Exhausted, they sprawled into the boat into a tangled heap. After pausing to catch their breaths and rub their sore muscles and bruises, they tried to stand up. Finding their balance and getting to their feet proved harder than they expected.

Knocking each other over more times than they could count, they added several more bruises to their respective collections. Finally, after much effort they managed to stumble upright. Holding on to anything they could find they made their way to the halyard and raised the sail. With the sail raised the boat stopped its tossing and evened out upon the water. Taking control of the wheel Mathew guided the boat away from shore. The wild tossing abated as the sailboat righted itself and turned away from the wind. The sails billowed out as the wind filled them propelling the vessel faster and faster away from shore. Pulling out his newfound compass, Mathew pointed the boat north and secured the tiller.

"Hey," Dillon said as he sat next to Mathew, "I don't mean to rain on our parade but what happens if we run into an alien patrol boat? They could blow us out of the water and we wouldn't stand a chance."

"We don't have a choice. We have to make it to New Hampshire and get our info to the Colonel. We're running out of time. Hopefully with the weather getting bad the aliens will stay out of the water. If not, we can always say we're fisherman and got thrown off course."

"Yeah, they'll believe that. We don't even have fishing poles or nets. They're stupid, but not that stupid," Dillon said sarcastically.

"Well, let's hope we don't run into anyone. We are going to have our hands full with this storm. By the way, what do we name our boat? My dad used to say that every boat should have a name." Even though it faithfully served its sailing master, it had a life of its own, his father used to say. With all its creaks, moans and groans, it ached for recognition and acknowledgment. Respect her and she will do her best to obey your wishes and forgive you your mistakes.

"How about the Royal Cheeseburger?" Dillon said, his mouth watering at the mention of his favorite food. Mathew heard his friend's stomach growl in hunger and false anticipation.

"Ha, ha, ha." Mathew laughed. "Royal Cheeseburger it is."

Mathew marveled at his friend's ability to relate everything to food, while disregarding the danger of their current situation. Dillon used to joke that he wanted to be a super ninja spy who masqueraded as a chef when he grew up. Like Peter Parker's photographer and Clark Kent's reporter alter egos, his would be that of a world-famous culinary genius. The dishes he would use to cloak his identity were often just as nauseating, as they were appetizing. Who else other than somebody who loved peanut butter with pickles and marshmallow fluff on a waffle would come up with a baked pork chop smothered in a foie gras olive tapenade and served with a side of pickled beets and roasted potatoes with drizzled gravy and goat cheese.

"Hold on a second," Mathew yelled. "I've got an idea." Shuffling forward on all fours like a monkey, he stuck his head through the open hatch, momentarily forgetting his fatigue. Lying flat he reached in with his arm and, after some squirming and grunting, removed an empty beer bottle. He crawled to the front of the boat, where he stood upright. His legs spread wide, assuming an official pose a crooked politician would envy, he announced, "As master of this ship, I officially christen thee the Royal Cheeseburger." He then smashed the bottle against the bow, breaking it in multiple pieces that washed away in the waves. Dropping the neck of the bottle over the gunwale, he made his way back. "Now it's official," he said, humoring his friend as he returned to his original seat.

"Touché, Admiral Wet Pants." Dillon giggled.

The Royal Cheeseburger heaved herself over a large wave. Her rigging creaked in protest. Standing at the wheel, half-awake, Mathew barely noticed the noise. But the soft rush of the spreading sail, the thrilling surge of the boat as it caught the stiff wind, told him the Royal Cheeseburger was holding her own. Keeping his eyes on the sail, trying to calculate their speed, he tried to keep his eyes open. He saw the shore to his left, his port side. He didn't see any other ships on the water. He didn't know if he should be elated or worried with the lack of other seafaring vessels.

Looking up at the darkening skies, he wondered if their luck had run out and they were sailing into trouble. It was uncommon for hurricanes this early in the year but not unheard of. Hurricane Sandy, termed the "storm of the century," was a category three storm that made landfall of the coast of North Carolina and then moved up the East Coast of the United States, causing close to a billion dollars in damage. Admonishing himself for his negativity and pessimism, Mathew forced his mind out of its self-imposed funk and resumed scanning the darkening horizon.

Mathew wondered about the information he had been entrusted with. It could change the direction of the rebel war. Perhaps they would never make it to their destination. The aliens knew something was abreast and their spies and confederates were out trying to gather any intel they could. The General would be extremely angry with his escape and would be trying to recapture him, just so he could save face. It didn't say much for their capabilities as world conquerors or do much for their fierce reputation when they couldn't detain, let alone find, a child.

As soon as they were on course, Mathew tried to get comfortable. His friend was already curled up on deck, fast asleep. They would reach their destination by morning if this wind held up. Judging by the increasing gales Mathew knew it was going to be a long night. But that they would make good time getting to New Hampshire if they didn't capsize and drown in the process.

Tomorrow morning! Mathew's heart raced as he thought about it. The fate of a nation depended on him getting his message to the right people. He was hungry, thirsty, soaked through and through, and scared, but he was resolved to complete his mission or die trying. He thought of his dad, dead; his mom, alone; Molly and all the friends he would never see again; and he thought of the millions of people who had died just for being human. As his eyelids grew heavy with fatigue, he hoped he was up to the task.

CHAPTER 19

• • •

AFTER A LONG RAIN-DRENCHED NIGHT, the boys neared the coast of New Hampshire. They desperately searched the shoreline for a place to land. The weather had cleared considerably and judging by the humidity, it was going to be another hot one. Not knowing the coastline, Mathew was hard pressed to make a decision. He feared hidden reefs as well as rocky shores. The Royal Cheeseburger, although seaworthy wasn't the strongest vessel on the water. The slightest damage to her hull would sink her in a heartbeat.

At ten o'clock they spotted a beach in the distance. It looked like a beach. They silently hoped it would meet their needs; they'd have to risk a landing regardless. They couldn't keep sailing up and down the coast. Sooner or later, they'd be spotted by an alien patrol.

Mathew said, "I'm going to steer for that cove. It's our best chance to land without drowning. What do you think?"

"Why you asking me? Do I look like a sailor? I'm lucky I haven't fallen over the side yet! What do I think?-- I think you better get us ashore, before I start eating the ropes. That's what I think! If I've said it once, I've said it a million times, if God wanted me this far offshore, he would have given me fins."

"Okay, okay. Chill. I'll do my best," Mathew said trying to adjust the sail and calculate his speed and distance so as not to overshoot his landing. Focused at the task at hand, he heard Dillon singing the McDonald's commercial fish song, over and over, while staring into the ocean. Hunger had made him delusional.

"Give me back that Filet-O-Fish. Give me that fish. Give me back that Filet-O-Fish. Give me that fish. What if it were you hanging up on this wall? If it were you in that sandwich, you wouldn't be laughing at all. Give me back that Filet-O-Fish. Give me that fish. Give me back that Filet-O-Fish. Give me that fish. What if it were you, hanging up on this wall? If it were you in that sandwich, you wouldn't be laughing at all."

When he was a few hundred yards from shore, Mathew swung the Royal Cheeseburger into the wind. The sail lost its shape, and Mathew raced to sheet it to the proper angle. He took everything into consideration--the current, the shift of the tide, the speed as he calculated his course. He had to keep the boat on course or else they'd miss the cove and beach and have to start over. Since he wasn't familiar with the tides in this area, he might not get another chance today.

"Here we go," he said more to himself than to his friend. The Royal Cheeseburger sailed through the water with a purity of the motion. His heart was pounding and skipping in rhythm with the waves. He stared at the approaching beach-line, hoping and praying there weren't any underwater reefs that would scuttle their craft.

The Cheeseburger sliced through the water like a warm knife through butter. Mathew was concentrating so hard on the beach and surrounding area that he didn't realize how shallow the water had become. Suddenly the boat's keel grated on the pebbles and rocks below the surface. With a sudden lurch they came to a complete stop, still twenty-five yards from shore. The boys were thrown off-balance, falling to the deck. The noise the boat made in the silence of the morning was deafening. Mathew swore.

"Quickly, let's get off this tub and into the trees," Dillon said. He hoisted the backpack over his head and jumped into the sea. "We made enough noise to wake the dead!"

Mathew joined him. Small waves rolled in at irregular intervals gently urging them toward the beach. Dripping, the boys slogged out of the water and onto the sand. They were both trembling with the chill and with heightened nerves. Looking around cautiously, they hurried toward the tree line. Nothing stirred but the slight breeze. Somewhere ahead was the rebel army waiting for their report.

They moved off silently away from the water. A road should lie somewhere ahead of us, Mathew thought.

Scrambling through the trees, they finally found the road. This would be part of the access to the beach. Farther along, it would join up with a major highway.

"Hold up, Dillon."

"What's up? Do you have any idea where we are?" Dillon asked as he scanned the horizon. Squinting, while covering his eyes with his hand, he peered through the forest canopy.

Mathew replied, "I think we need to go north, but first we have to find the main highway or what's even left of it. We should take a few minutes to rest, eat, and dry out. I'm starving. Plus, once we find the road, we have to move quickly and get to the Colonel. The aliens will be moving those weapons soon. We need to get them that information, if we are going to stand a chance at seizing them."

"All right, kimosabi. Me Tonto, you Lone Ranger, me follow your lead," Dillon said in his best Tonto voice. Laughing to himself, he continued, "I'm so funny, I slay myself."

"Yeah, yeah, you're a regular dragon slayer. Now let's find a place to rest. And if we meet any aliens, you can slay them with your humor, while I run away."

After moving a few yards deeper into the woods they sat down to rest. It was several hours later when Mathew woke up. At some point it had started raining. Mathew was cold and wet. Dillon was sleeping against a tree. It was time to get moving. They had a lot of ground to cover.

"Get up, you lazy bum," he joked while flinging a dry acorn at his friend. "Time to go."

"I'm up, I'm up," Dillon said, running his hand over his face and through his hair, trying to wipe away the sleep. "I'm hungry."

"Yeah, yeah, never heard that before," Mathew teased.

Picking up a stout branch the size of an old person's cane, he set off. His stomach grumbling, Dillon followed. They moved silently through the trees, hoping to come across a road or major highway they could follow.

It was well past noon as they made their way through the woods. Avoiding branches and thorny bushes for the past couple of hours hadn't put them any closer to their destination. Even the compass wasn't giving an accurate heading and Mathew had a feeling they had been traveling in circles. He was about to tell Dillon his suspicion when he heard a sound that didn't belong in the woods. Quickly dropping down, he waved to Dillon to do the same. Raising his finger to his lips, he motioned his friend to be quiet.

Dillon who was bringing up the rear, quietly made his way to his side. Looking around he didn't see anything to cause alarm. "What is it?" he whispered.

"I thought I heard something," Mathew responded, trying to listen for any further activity.

"What? Are you sure it wasn't your imagination?"

"I don't know for sure. I swear I heard Magarnese."

"Magar-what?" his friend asked, a confused look on his face.

"Magarnese. It's a long story. Just hang on a second, while I investigate." Mathew crept forward, trying to be as quiet as possible. Using all the stealth skills his dad and

Dillon had taught him over the years and all he had seen in movies and TV shows, he slunk forward slowly moving branches and leafy limbs out of the way. He had covered about twenty-five yards, when he came over a slight rise and saw the back end of an unmanned alien motorcycle craft hovering about six feet in front of him.

The machine was every gear heads dream. Mathew remembered the first time he had seen one. He has spent hours covertly examining this extraterrestrial technological marvel. Imagine a top of the line racing S1000RR BMW motorcycle crossed with a Yamaha XR Viper snowmobile. The thing was a work of art. Bred for power and maneuverability it could do zero to one hundred in less than three seconds and handle like a luxury sedan at the same time. Loaded with all manner of weapons, both recognizable and alien it was on every superheroes Christmas list. A multicolored display represented everything from fuel cell power to targeting and weapons analysis. The sleek lines and armor-plated body were topped with cushioned leather expandable swivel seats. This was especially helpful to the rear rider who rode facing backward during battle engagements. He was able to turn and maneuver his body freely, while pointing the large laser gun at anything and everything that caught his attention. The flared body design with protective wings allowed for protection of the rider's lower extremities if they took fire from below.

Dropping flat to the ground Mathew anxiously searched for the owners of the vehicle. There, about ten feet to his left, an alien was relieving himself against a tree. Mathew frantically searched for the alien's partner, knowing that the hovercraft required two riders to operate. One to drive and maneuver the machine and the other to operate the weapon on the back and provide the necessary counterbalance. Not able to locate the other rider, Mathew was about to backpedal back to Dillon when all of a sudden, his friend was next to him. Slapping his hand over Dillon's mouth before he could make a sound, he pointed to the alien urinating to his left. Dillon's eyes widened in shock. Slowly moving his hand from his friend's mouth, he motioned for them to fall back.

Just as they were about to retreat, the alien soldier who had just completed his business yelled out in his language. Not knowing what to make of this, the boys momentarily froze. The alien moved in their direction. Quickly dropping any pretext of stealth, they jumped to their feet, turned, and ran smack into the second alien who had snuck up behind them.

The impact sent all three sprawling to the ground. Dazed and confused they tried to process what had just happened, while recovering from their collision. The fallen Magar soldier bellowed in Magarnese, while trying to stand up. Regaining their wits, the boys jumped up and turned to run away but ran full tilt into his partner.

Knocking down the alien, the boys quickly ran through the copse of trees.

"Run, Dillon. We have to get out of here."

"Holy crap, that was intense. I think I peed myself," Dillon said, scrambling to keep up.

It wasn't long until the aliens recovered themselves and started to shoot at the boys. As the shots hit surrounding trees and laser beams scorched the ground at their feet, the boys dodged like frightened rabbits. They stayed close to the ground to make smaller targets. When a few seconds later, the shooting stopped, they paused to catch their breath.

"That was close. What do we do now?" Dillon wondered out loud. Suddenly crashing noises could be heard from their left. "Here they come again. You have to admit, they ain't very pretty but they are persistent."

"Follow me. I got a plan. Just try to be quiet," Mathew said, amazed that his friend could still joke at a time like this.

Creeping slowly back toward the road they spotted the alien vehicle hovering in the same spot.

"Do you think we lost them?" Dillon asked.

"I--I don't know," Mathew stammered. "I think so."

Suddenly a shot rang out, hitting the tree the boys were leaning against and spraying them with splinters, bark, and wood chips.

"Oh crap, here we go again," yelled Dillon as he dislodged himself from the tree and ran. Dodging left and right trying to avoid the occasional shot he made his way out of the tree line and into the clearing.

Dillon froze, halfway through the clearing he stopped frantically searching for Mathew. One second they were running away together the next he was alone. Had his friend tripped and fallen or was he hit by an errant shot and lying dead in the leaves and rock-littered ground? He was about to retrace his steps in hopes of finding his partner when all of a sudden he heard his name being called. Thinking it was his imagination, he continued looking in the direction from which they had fled.

"Dillon! Dillon! Over here!"

Following the direction of the voice calling his name with his eyes, he saw Mathew sitting upon the alien hovercraft pushing buttons with one hand and waving him over with the other. Changing direction he ran over to Mathew.

"What are you doing? We have to get out of here," he said looking at Mathew as if he had suddenly sprouted horns.

"Get on! This is our only chance," urged Mathew, pushing a button that made the alien vehicle come roaring to life.

"Are you crazy? Do you even know how to drive one of those things?" Dillon asked climbing aboard.

"Do you have a better idea?"

A shot rang out from the trees as the aliens emerged from under cover. "Alright dude, if we are going to go now would be the time," Dillon offered in way of motivation as more shots were fired their way.

"Hold on!" Mathew screamed as he pushed a large green handle forward.

The craft shot forward as if it were a raging bull just released from its pen. The vehicle swerved left to right as Mathew tried to gain control.

Hanging on to his friend's waist for dear life Dillon tried offering suggestions. "Try the purple button," he yelled above the roar. "Push the red one! That big white one, push that, push that!"

"Shut up and let me think," Mathew yelled. He reached up and pulled back the green handle, slowing the contraption to a more manageable speed. He then turned the steering wheel to the right and was surprised to feel the beast turn in that direction. In his elation he barely missed a tree that jumped out in front of them. Quickly turning the wheel to the left, he made it around the tree but still managed to smash the rear end into it.

"Oops, that's going to leave a mark," his friend commented from behind.

Ignoring the running commentary from the back seat Mathew focused on his driving. The vehicle automatically adjusted for the change in ground elevation. All he had to do was control his speed and steer. It's just like driving ATVs, he thought, remembering the endless hours he and Dillon had spent on trails with their fathers. Only difference was they wore helmets and pads and didn't have someone shooting at them.

"Where are we going?" his friend asked, looking over Mathew's shoulder. "And where did our friends go?"

"Don't know, but I bet they've called in reinforcements. Keep your eyes open."

Coming over a rise and steering around a huge tree, its trunk the width of a small car, they almost ran into their two pursuers. They ran down a steep embankment, trying to intercept them. They must have taken a shortcut or they're really fast runners Mathew thought. Swerving to avoid a collision, Mathew and Dillon crouched low in their seats as bullets buzzed over their heads. The few birds and wildlife in and on the trees scattered to safety.

Mathew increased his speed by pushing the green handle an inch forward. The vehicle whipped forward as if recognizing the danger the shooting represented. Mathew ignored the rest of the instrument panel, having a hard enough time avoiding the flying bullets and all those trees that kept popping up in front of him. Dillon was keeping his suggestions to himself for once, letting Mathew focus on his driving. Avoiding another tree Mathew yelled to Dillon to give him an update on the pursuing aliens.

"They're still coming and they look pissed! Can't you activate any weapons on this thing and just blast them. These things have so many capabilities. They're so bad--"

More shots rang out before Dillon could finish his thought. Bullets and lasers sprayed the surrounding area as the aliens fired their weapons again. "Oh crap," the boys said simultaneously as several bullets strafed the vehicle making it falter and sputter.

"We're hit," Dillon yelled noticing a gaping hole by his leg.

Mathew frantically tried to keep the bucking craft under control. He automatically pushed the green handle to its most forward position trying to coax as much speed from the dying machine as he could. All of a sudden they came to a steep incline. With nowhere to go but straight ahead, Mathew prayed it had enough power left to clear the hill in front of them. Leaning forward to minimize as much air resistance as possible, they boys held their breath as the vehicle continued to rise parallel to the ground as it tried to clear the hill. Thrashing and squealing, sputtering and jerking, the alien hovercraft barely flew over the crest before giving a tremendous groan, followed by a cough that killed all forward momentum. The vehicle screeched to a halt. Stopping as if hitting a concrete barrier, the vehicle dropped six feet straight to the ground, ejecting the boys several feet in different directions.

Dazed and bruised, the boys scrambled to their feet and stood looking at the burning mass of metal that had saved their lives.

"Come on, we have to get out of here before those freaks catch up," Mathew urged his friend as he retrieved the backpack that was hanging on a prickly bush. "This way."

Mathew ran away from the wreckage. Dillon followed limping slightly from a twisted ankle. The aliens would be upon them in no time, they had to put as much distance between them as possible. Always fleet of foot the boys ran through the woods ducking and dodging obstacles as they tried to cover as much ground as possible. It seemed like hours later, when the trees started to thin out and they could see blacktop in the distance.

CHAPTER 20

• • •

IT WAS DARK BEFORE THEY reached the highway, littered
with rocks of all sizes as well as massive holes, compliments of the alien's aircraft weapons. They could see multiple vehicles destroyed and scattered. Still standing under
the trees at the edge of the road, they stopped to catch
their breath. "I think we've lost them," Dillon said.

"We should take a break and then look for some sort
of sign to figure out where exactly we are. We can't be far
from the rebel camp and I don't want to head in the wrong
direction," Mathew added, thankful to be alive.

"My feet are killing me," Dillon complained. "I'm
hungry."

Before Mathew could reply, a pebble rattled somewhere in the distance. The sound came from their left. As
if reading each other's thoughts, both boys simultaneously
crouched down to present a smaller target. They held their
breath and waited.

They were about to move when they heard footfalls.
Mathew felt Dillon slip off into the darkness. Where was

he going? That crazy ninja stuff was going to get them both killed. He was going to beat Dillon senseless when he got his hands on him. Simmering with anger and worry, he was about to go after him when he heard muttering. Suddenly a large group of men materialized out of the night. Mathew recognized Dillon's voice.

"He's somewhere here, I'm positive. I just left him."

Even in the darkness, Mathew could make out his friend. He was standing next to a giant of a man. Mathew stared at this stranger, racking his brain to remember where he'd seen him before. Of course! He was the mountain he had run into at that bar on the harbor. What was he doing here?

"I'm here!" he said, rising from the ground and taking a few hesitant steps forward.

"Thank God! We've been looking for you two all over this coast," exclaimed the Jolly Green Giant. "We need to get back to camp as soon as we can. The colonel is mad with worry."

"How'd you know where we were?" Dillon asked.

"We got word from one of our scouts that they saw a boat trolling the shores. They reported two boys on the boat. When the Colonel got the message, he sent us out to retrieve you. Earlier we heard an explosion and expanded our search to this area. Some of the men thought they heard shots fired but weren't sure, so we investigated. We were about to vacate the area when Dillon showed up. We are to report back as soon as possible. If we leave now we can be there in a couple of hours."

"Do you have the message?" asked a second rebel as he chewed on an unlit cigar.

"Yes, we do. We need to get to the Colonel," Mathew said. The man's florid features, white hair and protruding belly resembled that of jolly old Saint Nick. Slap a Santa suit and fake beard on him and he'd make any mall proud.

The party split into two groups. The one that included the boys set out North; the other set off in the opposite direction. The giant explained that there were alien patrols in the area and they would keep an eye on them and provide a diversion if necessary.

"We need to get you to camp in one piece so you can report to the Colonel. It's imperative we have that information."

The giant led his group off the road a mile later, leading them up a hill. As they scrambled up the hillside, Dillon made his way next to Mathew. Together they trudged across the crest of the hill, through a thick grove of pine trees and scrub brush, each lost in his own thoughts. Suddenly, they could hear voices and sounds echoing throughout the trees. Camp!

The night was dark, occasionally punctured by the moon as it filtered through the leaves, illuminating their path. It was more than an hour later they broke into a clearing and the rebel camp. Mathew saw a figure creep across a stretch of grass heading toward them. He wondered if anyone else had seen him. He was about to speak when he heard the giant say, "It's us returning. Go check our six. Make sure we weren't followed."

"Aye, Sergeant," replied the sentry, heading off into the woods.

"That boy can sneak up on a rabbit and kiss its furry little butt when he puts his mind to it," a voice from the dark chuckled. Mathew and Dillon laughed out loud with the imagery. Several others including the giant joined them. The laughing continued more from relief that they had reached camp than from anything else.

"George, take the boys to the chow tent while I find the Colonel," said the giant as he veered off from the group.

"Now we're talking," exclaimed Dillon. "I can eat a horse!" he said his stomach growling in agreement.

Once they reached the mess tent, the boys rushed over to the chow line filling their plates. It had been so long since they had eaten real food that they heaped mounds of it onto their plates. They were waved over by a member of their rescue party.

"Make some room for the boys," he ordered his table mates.

Mathew and Dillon sat down hoping to put a dent in their plates, but they were quickly inundated with questions about their mission. Too tired to respond, Mathew let Dillon do all the talking while he savored his meal. Dillon regaled them with their adventures, improvising and exaggerating, while chewing the whole time. Having put on quite a show for the rebels in the dining hall, both with his rendition as well as his appetite, Dillon finished his meal and story with a loud and extremely satisfying burp. Mathew was surprised and impressed with his friend's oratory skills. His hunger was another matter altogether. Even though small in stature, Dillon had quite the prodigious appetite. Having seen him eat many times, Mathew was immune to his friend's insatiable appetite, but he was quite a hit with the rebels who went so far as to bet on if he would finish his foot tall pile of food. Not only did he finish, but he also went back for seconds and dessert. They had just finished when the Colonel walked in, followed by Sergeant Big as a House.

"Glad to see you boys. We were worried there for a while," the Colonel said with a smile. "Did you make contact with our informant?"

"Yes, sir," Mathew replied. "Would you like us to report what we were told," he asked, looking around for Dillon. He saw his friend passed out, head on the table.

"Why don't you follow me to my tent, Mathew?" the colonel ordered. "We'll let Dillon sleep, unless you think we need him in on our meeting?"

"No, sir. I have all the information you need."

With the Colonel leading the way out, they made their way around what was the motor park and into an isolated cabin. Mathew followed hardly able to keep his eyes open, almost tripping over his own feet on several occasions. When they entered the cabin the rebel commander lit a lantern on a table and turned toward him.

In the headquarters the Colonel said, "Okay Mathew, let's hear your report. Start from the beginning and don't leave anything out. I know you are tired, but please include as much detail as possible."

Mathew had just started his narrative when several other people entered the cabin quietly to hear his tale. When he finished the room was silent. The men looked at him with awe and pride. He felt his cheeks getting red, as they suddenly all praised him and Dillon on their success.

"Colonel, if we can capture those weapons, we can go a long way in our fight against the Magars," said a man to Mathews's right.

"I know, Sam, but we have to think this through and come up with a foolproof plan before we attempt anything. We will only get one chance at this and we can't afford to fail." Looking over at Mathew, he saw that he was on the verge of collapse. "Mathew, go get some rest. Tiny, help him to find a cot. We will be debriefing you and Dillon again tomorrow."

As he left the cabin, he almost laughed when he realized that the Colonel had called the giant sergeant Tiny. Tiny? For some reason he found this hilarious. Who would have thought?

They entered another tent, this one full of sleeping rebels. Mathew was so tired his knees buckled. Tiny picked the first bunk in front of him off the ground with one hand, and dumped its snoring occupant to the floor. Righting the cot, he gently lifted Mathew off the floor and placed him in it as if he were a small child.

"Sleep," he said as he casually opened the door and threw the complaining previous occupant out of the tent.

Mathew was asleep before his head hit the pillow.

To be continued....

Made in the USA
Coppell, TX
11 May 2021